BILLIONAIRE SECOND
CHANCE

BILLIONAIRE SECOND CHANCE

A Forced Proximity Secret Baby Romance

BLAKELY STONE

Foreword

An explosive one-night stand with years and miles dividing us.

Only one thing keeps us connected...the son he knows nothing about.

I rent an extravagant beach house on secluded Duck Island to regroup after my divorce. Surprising us both, billionaire owner Grayson Sterling is staying there, too.

Come to find out, his assistant has been Airbnb-ing his retreat without his knowledge.

Gratefully he honors the reservation since I have nowhere to go.

As long as I agree to share it with him.

One steamy night by the fire is all that is between us.

Or so we thought.

Fast forward six years and fate reunites us on the same beach.

The insane chemistry is still there, but life isn't so simple anymore.

The truth I've kept from him since that fateful night threatens to break free.

There is no hiding the resemblance between Grayson and my son.

ONE

Grayson

Thursday, March 7th, 2019

East Hampton Airport (KHTO / HTO)

7:22 am EST / 4:22 am PST

WE PULL onto the tarmac in a sleek Lincoln Towncar. I am still amped up from my after two am victory, if still a little groggy from only three and a half hours of sleep.

A handshake and a letter of intent on a > $2B flagship building in Manhattan. That makes me the fucking Mac Daddy. I am now the broker and soon-to-be owner of the most expensive commercial real estate deal in the city.

I initially planned to stop at $2.3B, but they wouldn't budge from 2.45, and I really wanted that Madison Avenue address. Finally, at two in the morning or shortly after, we all wore each other down to a compromise that made it work for both sides.

We close in four weeks, and I am happy to no longer have that hanging over my head. The rest of the transaction will be up to the lawyers and Goldman Sachs. With my signature on the closing docs next month for the coups de gras, of course.

My usual driver, Olivier, is already in Denver waiting for my arrival, so Christian is driving me this morning. Once the car is in park near the jet, he steps out to get my hanging bag and roller board.

My phone buzzes as my hand rests on the shiny, cold door handle to open it. It's Thomas Earhardt with Coastal Horizon Development Group. I answer quickly, eager for an update. "What's the word, Thomas?"

"Glad I caught you, Grayson. Is there any chance you could fly in today for a sit down with the city planner about our development first thing tomorrow morning? We have been trying to get in with him for months, so I didn't want to miss the opportunity if you can make it."

Years of negotiations on a groundbreaking mixed-use development in Virginia Beach, and it is all riding on this dumbass government rubber stamp. We would have already broken ground if they hadn't been stringing us along for the better part of seven months. Being on the East Coast already makes the decision to change my plans a no-brainer. I can reschedule Denver.

"Sure, Thomas. I wouldn't miss it. I'm in New York, so I will switch my flight. What time is he thinking tomorrow?"

"Fantastic. I knew I could count on you. Let me call him back to get an exact time. Plan on first thing in the morning. I think this will be it, so we can start rolling. I'll text you the time once I talk to him."

I step out into the cold morning, pulling my cashmere trench coat snugly around my chest to shield me from the biting wind. The sun still isn't entirely up, and the sky is gray. It will be a cold, dull spring day in the northeast.

I let Christian know I am changing the destination but that he can still load my things onto the jet. I walk into the evoJet office across the blacktop, my toes feeling the cold asphalt through my leather soles.

I change my flight to Norfolk, Virginia, the closest airport to the Outer Banks, which is where my beach house is. And then I call Claire.

Claire is the assistant to my assistant, Everly.

Everly is on vacation, so I have to make do without her. It's a thorn in my ass when she is out because she knows what I need before I do and takes care of it. Without her, I do it myself or walk someone else through it, which takes more time anyway.

"Claire," I bark, eager to have all the logistics in order and irritated that I have to do all of the detail work to put it in place.

"Good morning, Sir. Everything okay in New York?" She sounds groggy. Everly would never answer the phone, sounding like she had just rolled over in her bed. My irritation is growing. I don't do well with change and have zero patience for incompetent employees.

"I need you to arrange a car and driver for me at the Norfolk airport immediately. This morning, have someone meet me there at nine, East Coast time. Olivier won't be able to make it in time, but let him know the change and have him come out there for the rest of the week. I'm changing my plans and am flying there instead of Denver."

"Oh, okay," she stammers, clearing her throat. Drink your damn coffee, for Christ's sake. I don't care that it is only four in the morning there. When your boss is on the East Coast, you need to be up and ready on East Coast time.

"I've taken care of the flight plans, but I need you to ensure everything in Virginia and North Carolina is set. The beach house should be ready and the refrigerator stocked. I'll be staying there until Tuesday."

"But Mr. Sterling, I--"

Goddammit. The only thing I should hear back is the affirmative. I cut her off. "I don't have time for this, Claire. Just make it happen." I disconnect, not in the mood to hear her protestations.

―――

NORFOLK INTERNATIONAL AIRPORT *(ORF)*

9:51 am EST

I'M SERIOUSLY about to lose my shit. I understand why Olivier couldn't arrive in time with the last-minute change. But someone should be here to get me, goddammit. I specifically instructed Claire. There was no ambiguity in what I said.

Instead, I am standing here with my thumb up my ass trying to figure out how I am going to get to the Outer Banks. I pay people to worry about this shit, so I don't have to.

"Where the fuck is Claire?" I say out loud to no one in particular as I walk back into the small private jet office. She hasn't called me to give me an update. When I just tried her cell, it went straight to voicemail. Completely unacceptable.

Bloody hell if I am going to sit around at Monarch Air's sorry excuse for a lounge waiting on anyone. Someone is going to lose their job over this.

But for now, I have to drive myself. I should be relaxing in the back seat, taking in the picturesque ride.

Who am I kidding? I never take time to appreciate the landscape.

But that is beside the point. The last thing I want to do is get behind the wheel and drive the two hours it will take to get there. Especially after the late night and early morning I have already had.

———

10:46 *am EST*

I THROW my shit into the back seat of whatever pathetic rental the assistant at Monarch could round up at the airport on short notice. I can't believe I'm stuck driving this ugly ass sedan for the next two hours.

Claire clearly has not learned how to walk and chew gum at the same time. You would have thought I told her she needed to coordinate the Pope's visit. She seemed so flustered.

I can feel the tension coiling tighter inside of me, my irritation seeping out of my pores.

My lack of sleep last night is most definitely not helping the situation.

Thinking about last night's win does little to calm my nerves right now. I might as well be driving through Skid Row with the amount of rage and resentment that is swarming inside of me. Every scenic mile seems to amplify the frustration that I've been nursing since I rushed to get to the airport this morning to get to Denver by nine on virtually no sleep.

The car's tires hum on the open road. The monotony of the thick trees and level ground threatens to lull me. I struggle to keep my eyes open. The fatigue from yesterday's relentless day and the early morning today weighs heavily on my eyelids. And a moment comes when I want nothing more than to give in to the deliciousness of slumber. If I just close my eyes for a moment, just one moment…

———

11:52 *am EST*

That one moment must have turned into two or three or four, and I find myself jolted back into consciousness by the thump-thump of my tires on the rumble strips on the edge of the road. My heart is racing, and my mind is still trapped in the nightmare about a board meeting and the realization that I forgot to wear pants, trying to figure out a way to get out of there with no one noticing I am business up top and party below.

The tires screech, and I swerve the car dangerously close to the shoulder. My stomach leaps into my throat. Time slows. A paralyzing fear grips me as I battle to regain control.

I manage to correct myself just in time, the feeling of imminent disaster still at the forefront of my mind. My pulse pounds through my entire body. My hands are trembling so I grasp the wheel tighter to steady them.

Sweaty fistfuls of the hard, molded leather of the steering wheel are squeezed between my palms and fingers as I try to catch my breath. My knuckles are bright white, and the blood flowing past my wrist has officially halted.

The narrow escape is a stark reminder of my own vulnerability. No matter how wealthy or powerful I might be, I am not immune.

"This is why I need a fucking driver," I mutter irritatedly, jumpstarting my anger all over again.

My fear and annoyance in equal measure simmering just at the top of my throat, begging for a release. I yell out and hit the steering wheel. "Dammit," I grumble, the words bellowing out through gritted teeth. I check the *Waze*. Christ. I still have just over an hour.

I can do this. The adrenaline alone should be enough to get me through the next hour, at least. I take a sip of the ridiculously marketed sports drink du jour I got at the Monarch convenience store before stomping out of there. It is supposed to keep you awake, increase your stamina, and help you win friends and influence people. It tastes like dog shit. I should have known.

As I cross the border into North Carolina, I scowl at the cheerful road signs welcoming me to the state. What is there to be cheerful about?

The quaint towns with inviting storefronts and roadside stands don't elicit any warm feelings for me. Nor does the bright sunshine that is cutting through the windshield.

I have no interest in stopping for fresh produce or local crafts. I just want to reach Duck, my house, my bed, and rest up before my meeting tomorrow morning back in Virginia Beach.

I reach for my phone propped up in the cup holder. The GPS arrow is following along the US-17 line on the screen. I decide that talking on the phone will help my mind and body stay awake. I pull up Olivier's number and press send.

"Good morning, Sir," he answers on the second ring. Finally, someone on the West Coast is up and able to talk to me.

"Not much good about it, but I appreciate the sentiment. I trust you got the message that I made a last-minute change and will be in Virginia and North Carolina instead of coming to Denver."

"Yessir, I got a text from Claire. But she didn't give me any details, so I have been waiting for her to tell me the details before making my change."

I don't know how she got this job. She is painfully inadequate.

"Can you get to North Carolina for a meeting tomorrow morning? I will need to be in Virginia Beach by ten thirty, so we will need to leave the Outer Banks no later than eight."

"Yes, I think I can swing that. I will arrange a flight now." The best news so far today. Thankfully, I won't be doing this god-forsaken drive again.

"Great. Thanks for being on it. Touch base tonight and let me know everything is set."

"Ten-Four."

I roll down the window. The air is considerably warmer here than this morning in New York. But there is still a crispness in the air. I love springtime here. I let the wind lick my face, blowing a little extra life into this tired body.

The anticipation of reaching my beach house and the promise of solitude are the only things that keep me going right now. It's a fleeting sensation, quickly overshadowed by everything weighing on me. I try to let it all slip away and focus on getting there in one piece.

Just over thirty minutes now. I got this.

TWO

Hollis
_____

Duck, North Carolina

12:56 PM *EST*

I FEEL the warmth beaming down from almost directly overhead. The cool air and the bright sun, in perfect measure, are good for my soul. I throw the smooth shell I have been manipulating between my fingers. I follow it as it bounces several times before finding its new resting place in the sand.

I marvel as the waves lap in and back out to sea, the gentle monotony soothing my soul.

"Ready to go up to the house, Mr. Bojangles?" I ask my dog, who is lying beside me. He rolls on his back in the sand in answer. We've been recovering from our long stroll down the beach and back for the past 45 minutes. I push up from the sand in front of the beach house I rented for the week.

I am in a bit of a drowsy lull after the rest following our walk. I need to get up and move, or I risk falling asleep right here where I sit.

I rise languidly and brush off the wet sand from my backside. The sensation of the grit sticking to my palms provides a simple pleasure.

My tummy grumbles. It is time for some lunch. I dropped my car off down the street yesterday when we got into town for some much-needed love, so we will have to find somewhere around here to walk to. My phone is upstairs. I will google somewhere close when we get up there.

My toes curl into the sand with each step, feeling the wet, hard, but forgiving ground pushing back at me as we approach the deck steps leading to the house.

I love this beach and this town. Even the air I breathe is better here.

My divorce was finalized yesterday, and we came right away. I reserved the house over three months ago when I first learned the date of reckoning. This is my safe place. My refuge from the storm. I knew immediately that this was where I needed to come as soon as we signed the papers.

Bowen, my now ex-husband, and I tried to make it work. But in the end, there was no more love there between us. I couldn't wait to shake the dead weight of being married to him. And yesterday, when I completed my final signature, sealing our divorce, it truly felt like I shed a hundred and fifty pounds.

I am happy with what I got from the marriage: Mr. Bojangles, my beloved snuggle bunny Golden Retriever. Bowen kept everything else, including the Weber Grill and the framed, signed wedding day poster that probably still hangs in the hall of the home he also got to keep.

On the bright side, the house was mortgaged to the hilt, so he gets that, too. The mortgage, that is. We might have had to bring money to the closing table if we forced the sale. There is no equity there for him to buy me out. I have no sentimental feelings connected to that house, so it was not a hard decision for me.

Good riddance. I mean that in the warmest way possible. Bowen isn't a bad guy. He just wasn't my guy, and I wasn't his girl. It was time for a fresh start and a clean slate.

Mr. Bojangles and I will be just fine, "Right, Buddy?" I ruffle the soft, red fur behind his ears as we get to the top of the wooden stairs. I came out on top with this one. He looks at me adoringly, his tongue out and his light brown eyes filled with love. The most loyal and loving male I have ever had in my life is right here with me in my favorite place. Our fresh start is already looking up.

We take a seat on the wooden swing before going in. I rub my bare feet together, trying to shake all of the sand off before going in.

As we sit on the wood deck, watching the waves and the occasional walker stroll by, I can't help but feel a slight melancholy. I haven't been in love with Bowen for many years, but it still feels sad that a part of my life is over. That idea that I would very likely never see or talk to him again is a bit odd. But I will get used to it. There is now nothing left to bind us together.

We weren't able to have children. It is a blessing in disguise now, in hindsight, but when we were going through it, it was a bitter reality we faced together. We saw a fertility specialist, but they were unable to figure out why. We just couldn't get pregnant. After we declined fertility treatment, we gave up on trying and figured if it happened, it would happen. It never happened.

You have to have sex to get pregnant.

Bowen and I met in college at William & Mary. He played soccer, and I thought he was the coolest dreamboat I had ever seen. The sex in college was amazing. That faded slowly day by day after graduation. The steady decline of the quality of sex together was unrecognizable until, one day, I was just laying there like a starfish until it was over.

Starfishing. My new verb.

After college, he landed a coveted role as a computing research scientist at Quantum Innovations Lab, a tech company located in Raleigh, NC. He asked me to come with him.

I was an aspiring author, so I could live anywhere. The idea of moving to a new state with the man I thought was the love of my life was exciting. I had never lived anywhere outside of the state of Virginia. And Raleigh was still close enough to home to give me a little extra security. There was something to be said for knowing that I could drive back home in a few hours if need be.

He asked me to marry him at our tiny downtown Durham, North Carolina rental. Life was simple then, and the world was our oyster. We married shortly after that, just before he started grad school at NC State.

Between his demanding work and his Ph.D. studies, we had little time to nurture our new marriage. I went further into my introverted hole and would spend eighty hours a week writing. I suppose it was good for my writing but bad for stoking the marriage sparks.

I think we weren't even a year into our marriage when I came to the realization that, quite possibly, our best years were already behind us. I was twenty-three at the time, and that thought was depressing for me. But I didn't know what to do about it, so we kept doing what we were doing, growing apart.

We were merely roommates by the time he finished his dissertation and doctoral capstone — ships passing in the night.

Many nights, he would stay at his office until the wee hours of the morning. I used to try to stay awake for him, but soon enough, I would go to bed when I was ready. And there were many nights that I didn't even know when he got home, if he got home at all. Most of the time, I didn't even know he was sleeping beside me until I got up the following day.

We thought trying for a baby would bring us the connection we both desired. When that didn't happen, there wasn't much left for us to hope for as a couple. He was furthering his career, and I was writing. We lived in two separate worlds in the same over-leveraged house.

We tried therapy. We took vacations. We scheduled date nights. We even got a dog. None of it really moved the needle except to keep driving the wedge further and further between us.

Neither of us has any animosity for the other. What we had was apathy. A good three or so years of it. If he had put up a fight to keep Mr. Bojangles, we might have had fighting words. But he surrendered my faithful friend without protest.

He knows full well that Mr. B., a gift from me to Bowen two Christmases ago, is my only constant companion. And he also knows that I am Mr. B's person, even though he was technically his dog. A suggestion from our therapist. The best advice we got after over six thousand dollars and a year's worth of weekly visits.

As soon as we enter the house, I realize how famished I am. "How about we go into town to grab some lunch, huh, Buddy?" My stomach grumbles again at the mention of lunch, and Mr. Bojangles does a little tap dance on the glossy wood floors. The gulls are singing, and the temperature and sunlight are perfect. It's going to be a good day.

THREE

Grayson
---

3 N Baum Trail

Duck, NC 27949

1:12 PM *EST*

I FINALLY PULL into my oasis from the crazy world. Of all of my homes across the country, including the one off the coast of Italy, this is the one that is my true refuge.

The Outer Banks is quite possibly the one place on earth that is still mostly undeveloped. It is my life's work to exploit these types of areas. But this place is the exception. I will leave it unspoiled, and I will protect it from development. Protect it from people like me.

My career as a real estate developer sort of fell into my lap unexpectedly. I had always planned to be an architect, like my grandfather, who was renowned in his field. I was very close to him growing up in Bend, Oregon. I admired him for many reasons, but his clout always impressed me wherever he went.

I went to Stanford, where I got a Bachelor of Science in Civil Engineering. My main focus was to immerse myself in courses related to design, urban planning, and real estate economics. Those courses opened my eyes to other possibilities within that realm.

After completing my undergraduate degree, I decided to gain practical experience in the construction industry before starting the architecture program at USC. Then, I ended up taking on a project manager role for a renowned construction firm in L.A. During those early years, I developed a deep understanding of construction processes, land acquisition, and project management.

The big pivotal move into real estate development happened when I recognized the potential for profit in transforming underutilized properties into valuable assets. Drawing from my experience in construction and a keen eye for identifying prime locations, I began investing in small-scale residential development projects. My first ventures, although modest in scope, proved to be successful.

Driven by ambition and a relentless work ethic, I decided to launch my own real estate development company, Sterling Development Group, rather than pursue my advanced degree in architecture. I was already making close to a million dollars a year by the time I was two years in. And people were already deferring to me, just like they had to my grandfather. It was hard to justify quitting that success train to take on debt and start down a completely different path.

The sunlight flickers as it filters through the tall trees and occasional clearings. I pull the visor down to shield the glare. The stark difference between the gray morning in New York, the tall buildings piercing the skyline, and the sunny, natural horizon here is striking. The stretches of live oaks and marsh grass make me feel like I'm in a scene in a Pat Conroy novel.

At the beginning of my career, I focused on acquiring underperforming properties, redeveloping them, and selling or leasing them at a significant profit. This business model allowed me to gain valuable insights into the real estate market, negotiate deals, and build a network of industry contacts.

With a few successful projects under my belt, Sterling Development Group grew, and I began to diversify my portfolio, doing bigger and riskier deals. I expanded into commercial real estate, partnering with investors and financial institutions to secure funding for larger and larger projects.

My ability to spot opportunities, coupled with a strategic approach to property acquisition and development, my relationships in the lending community, and my success all contributed to my rapid ascent in the industry.

The familiar streets, trees, and landmarks give me pause. We are getting close. A calm washes over me.

The sleepy fishing towns leading up to Duck are the heart and soul of this part of the country. I've never liked fishing myself. But the happiness I get from being in this place and around people who live and breathe the fishing lifestyle is something I can't explain. It just is.

Over the years, my company has thrived, and I have consistently made shrewd investment decisions. I expanded my real estate empire beyond California little by little, each new deal a bit further east. And within the last few years, I have ventured into all major U.S. cities. Now, nobody can deny that I'm a nationwide industry player.

My vision and sheer dedication to dominating have made me a self-made billionaire, a status I am quite proud of. Without bragging too much, I am one of the most prominent real estate moguls in the country. Maybe the most prominent.

Here, on my three acres that touches both the Albemarle Sound and the Atlantic Ocean, I can take off my asshole hat. I can let my cares and stresses blow out with the ocean wind. As soon as I park the car, I feel my steely, cold anxiety fade, and the warmth of the comfort of this place fills me.

Home.

My house sits on twenty-foot-high stilts as per the building zoning here. A small studio apartment for staff is on the ground level, built under the back portion of the house. I pull the car in under the house up to the apartment. The front bumper faces the ocean but is hidden behind the horizontal slats that cover the crawl space area, making sure not to expose myself to the neighbors.

First of all, I don't want any of my overly friendly neighbors to know I am here. The last thing I need is people "popping in," as they sometimes like to do around here. I might admire and even have affection for the people who make this place so special, but I really don't want to be friends with any of them.

And second of all, I would prefer not to be caught dead driving a bitch car like a BMW. That reminds me, I need to make sure Claire gets someone to come pick up this piece of shit. It's devaluing my real estate just being parked under my house.

I grab my roller board, hanging bag, and my briefcase and exit the car. The smell of the North Carolina beach fills my soul. I call the elevator down, and I step in and inhale the familiar mildew smell that comes with it. Oddly comforting.

I press the button for the second floor, my primary bedroom, bypassing the mudroom on the main floor.

The Prime drink and adrenaline got me here in one piece, but now I hear my Purple mattress calling me. I suddenly feel drained again and plan to go straight to the bed, not even taking a shower first.

I walk into my bedroom and note immediately that it's in disarray. I can't even think about this additional dereliction of duty on Claire's part. We will seriously discuss replacing her as soon as Everly returns next week. First, though, I must sleep. Then I will deal with it.

Oh, how I love this view of the ocean. The whole ocean side of the house on the second floor is covered in windows. My bedroom has a massive room with its own balcony. Usually, all of the natural light would be good for my psyche, but at the moment, all I want is darkness.

I push the button for the automatic blinds, and the room goes black within seconds. I fall onto the down puff, kicking off my Gucci loafers. The feathers and linen swallow me whole, hugging me and snuggling me to sleep. Sleep that I have been craving since I was so rudely awakened by my early alarm this morning.

FOUR

Hollis

1:49 pm EST

I ENTER the front door with a full belly and aching legs. Between our hour-long walk this morning and our walk to and from town for lunch, my dogs are barking. I fill a clean bowl of water for Mr. Bojangles, whose tongue hangs from the side of his mouth. He plops down on the hardwood floor beside the bowl and laps up almost all the water from that position, puddles sloppily going everywhere on him and the floor.

I hang his leash on the back of the chair by the front door and lower myself on the salmon-colored sofa facing the ocean, my eyelids heavy. I want to go out to the hammock on the porch and take a nap, ideally situated in the afternoon sun. But I don't even have the energy to walk outside. I lay down right where I fall and close my eyes for just a moment.

———

2:58 PM *EST*

I AM startled awake by a bumping noise directly above me. I am frozen to my spot, confident that those sounds are footsteps on the wood floor on the second story. Mr. Bojangles is alert, sitting with his ears pricked, confirming that the sound wasn't just something from my dream.

My heart is beating out of my chest. My entire body is completely awake. My mouth is dry, and my brain is trying to think of what to do. I am more aware than ever that I am all alone with no car, and I am freaking out a little.

I realize I've been asleep for over an hour. How did I sleep that long? I was out cold, so I suppose someone could have slipped by me. But I find it hard to imagine someone could get in without Mr. Bojangles noticing.

Besides the occasional knocking above, the house is deathly silent. The afternoon sun is blaring in, making a warm spot on the sofa at my feet. Dust bunnies float in the air, illuminated by the streaks of bright light slicing through the room.

Mr. Bojangles stands up, and I realize he senses my distress. He might be the least ferocious dog on the planet, but he makes a formidable statement with his eighty-five-pound stature and blockhead.

A toilet flushes. There is no doubt about it. Someone other than myself is in the house. House settling doesn't make the commode spontaneously flush. I feel my back pocket, looking for my phone. Shit. It's on the entry table. I must have set it there when we walked in.

I slowly get up and tiptoe to the front door to retrieve it. It is my only weapon besides Mr. Bojangles. Neither of which will do a thing to protect me if this robber or murderer or whatever is up there comes down here right now with a weapon.

My plan is to grab my phone, get Mr. Bojangles, and run outside. We will run as fast as we can down the street while dialing 911. My flight or fight is hardcore flight. I am a big, fat wimp, just like my trusty companion. And I am totally okay with that.

On my third step, the wood floor creaks. I pause as if I just stepped on a booby trap, checking to make sure no one has been alerted by it.

Just then, Mr. Bojangles makes a B-line up the stairs. Oh, God. No. What is he doing?! What should I do?

I am in sheer panic mode.

If this person has a gun, they will shoot my dog before they ever realize that all he will do is lick them to death. Why does he feel like he has to save the day? I am filled with dread. My head is going to explode. I want to curl into a ball and cry. But I can't leave him and save myself. I've got to get to the phone.

I hear the loudest, most resounding bark I have ever heard from him, followed by a guttural growl. A bark that says he will rip someone's leg off if he has to. A bark that does not betray that he is a big, red teddy bear.

At that, I dash for the phone, no longer hampered by the fear of making a sound. Whoever is in this house is now fully aware that they are not alone. Mr. Bojangles has made that clear.

I dial 911 and head towards the stairs.

"Get the fuck away from me, you beast!" I hear booming from a room upstairs. A loud bang follows.

I freeze. Was that a gun firing? Mr. Bojangles is growling, so he is still alive and feisty. I think it was just a door slamming, but I can't be sure. Everything sounds like a battle cry right now.

More blood-curdling growls. The sound is almost constant. The slam of a door. This time, I am sure it is a door. My heart literally feels like it will beat out of my chest. The lump in my throat is so big it makes it hard for me to swallow.

I hear Mr. Bojangles' paws scrape on something. I do not hear a gunshot or a whimper, so I run up the stairs, hopefully to save him. I am running into unknown danger to save the only being I care about in this world.

"Mr. Bojangles! Get over here right now!" All of the blackout shutters are drawn, so I can hardly see him. The only light in the room is coming from the hallway behind me, and a thin line of light beams from the bottom of the closed bathroom door.

I can barely see, but it is evident that the bed has been slept in. A blazer is on the suit rack just inside the bedroom door, and a pair of fancy shoes is beside the bed. Is this some kind of bougie squatter or something?

Whatever it is, we need to get out of here now. He could have a fancy Swiss army knife or something.

"Get over here right now!" I whisper yell with the sternest face I can muster. I know the bad guy knows we are here, but for some reason, I don't feel comfortable straight-up yelling. If I can just keep him in the bathroom until we get out of here, I think everyone will be better for it.

Mr. Bojangles keeps his eyes and head fixed on the closed door. He does not seem to be backing down no matter how stern my whisper yell is. I tiptoe toward him, hoping I can somehow pull his hairy, enormous body down the stairs with me.

Don't be a hero, Mr. Bojangles, I tell him with my cocked head and beat-red face. He is not taking my cues.

When I get close to him, I can feel his growl. The volume is lower, but the baritone booms through the floors. I know this dog, and he wouldn't hurt a flea. But this guy, or girl, doesn't know that. He looks and sounds like a ferocious animal.

I am not going to lie. I am even a little frightened of him at this moment. I'm impressed.

"Come on, Buddy. Please, come with me," I whisper, tears streaming down my cheeks. I have never felt so helpless or so scared. I don't think I will survive if anything happens to this dog.

His growling stops, and he finally seems willing to come with me. I grab his thick leather collar and tread softly back toward the bedroom door. His claws click-click with each step. I knew I should have had him groomed before we came here.

The door creaks open, and I see a bright blue eye peering at me from inside the bathroom. I pull Mr. Bojangles harder, trying to put as much distance between me and the person on the other side of that door.

Just then, I hear a lady's voice coming through the phone in my hand. I completely forgot I had called 911. I must not have heard her answer through all the commotion and stress.

"Can you hear me? I have you pinged at 3 N Baum Trail in Duck. Is that correct? I have already dispatched an officer to your home. Please confirm that you can hear me and that you are safe."

I'm feeling somewhat safer knowing that the police are on the way and that I have someone on the other end of the phone. Still, I put the phone to my ear and whisper, "There is a man in my house. I am at 3 N Baum Trail. Please send someone immediately. We are unharmed, but I don't know what is going to happen. Please tell them to hurry."

FIVE

Grayson

3:03 pm EST

"YOU HAVE GOT to be fucking kidding me," I say through the crack, my bare foot jammed against the door in case that giant wildebeest lunges at me again. "Some stranger is in *your* house? Who the fuck are you, and why are you in *my* house!?"

I honestly cannot believe my life today. Two hours of sleep, a botched car service, a near-death experience on the ride here, and now I have some lunatic woman and her attack dog in my one place of sanctuary in this world. I seriously can't win for losing today.

"Yes, ma'am, he is talking to me, but I don't know who he is. My dog has planted himself, and I can't pull him down the stairs. I can't leave him here. Please hurry."

Is this crazy woman actually calling the police on me in my own home? I have heard of scenarios like this in California, where squatters take over peoples' homes while they are away and refuse to leave. The laws there are so tenant-friendly there that it is nearly impossible to get them out. But now this is happening in sleepy, coastal NC towns, too?! For crying out loud, these people will stop at nothing!

A loud boom emanates from downstairs. Is there a whole band of them?! Are these people robbing me? I have more money than God, and I am up here locked in the bathroom without a weapon or even a phone. A hostage in my own home, held up by a petite lady and her wooly mammoth.

"Police!" Someone yells from downstairs. Relief covers me. "Is anyone in the house? If you can hear me, please make yourself known. We're here to help. Stay where you are and keep the line open with the 911 operator if you can."

"Please come upstairs," the crazy lady yells down to them from my bedroom, keeping me locked in the bathroom. "We are all up here. I am renting this house, and my dog and I just came home from a walk. This man must have come in while we were gone. I can't pull my dog down, and I can't just leave him here."

Three officers come into the room with their weapons drawn directly at the two-inch crack in the door. Right at my left eye. My dominant eye.

"Sir, come on out of the bathroom with your hands up."

I open the door slowly, and the dog makes another lunge at me. Thank God the lady is holding his collar, but the dog almost pulls her with him. There are two cops, one man and one woman, both of them with weapons pointed directly at my head. The third is hanging back in the hall, his weapon also directed at my head.

Three's a charm.

I reach both of my hands out of the door crack. Then, I open it wide enough for my whole body to emerge. I want to make it clear that I am unarmed. If anyone gets shot, it should be that fucking dog.

"This is my house. This lady is a nutjob. I don't know who she is or why she is here. And that dog almost killed me. Arrest her and put that goddamned dog down." All of this I say with my hands up in the air. My words seem to lose all gravitas in my current stance.

The third police officer approaches the door with a gun still drawn, still not speaking a word. She holsters her weapon and asks the crazy lady to come downstairs with her. The dog finally seems to be willing to go with her instead of drooling over taking a bite out of my nuts.

His tail wagging, long hair fanning as it moves side-to-side, you would think he was just the friendliest dog you ever met. The Eddie Haskel of dogs. He is totally putting on an act for the cops, as if he didn't just trap me in my own home, teeth bared and ready for attack.

The male policeman comes over to me and pats me down, making sure that I am unarmed. As if I would stay locked up in that bathroom if I could have ended it all with a single shot. I am not a fan of guns anyway, but I guess they don't know that.

"Sir, I need you to remain where you are, and I am going to put you in handcuffs while we try to figure out what is going on here. We received a call about an intruder, and we're here to investigate. Please identify yourself and tell me what you're doing here?"

I hope they are putting handcuffs on that bitch, too. This is humiliating and infuriating. My blood is boiling.

"Officer, this is my home. I own this house. And I have owned it for almost ten years now." I am short of breath as I explain. No matter how deep of a breath I take, I don't feel I have enough oxygen to get it all out.

"And I owned this lot for years before that. It is not my primary home, but I spend a lot of time here. Ask any of the neighbors. They all know me. I do not know who that woman is. And she does not have permission to be here."

My breathing is heavy and rapid. You would have thought I just returned from a run if you didn't know any better. My hair is damp, and sweat is evident on my upper lip and forehead. I feel like I need to take a seat.

"May I please sit down on the bed?"

"Sure, have a seat. Is there any way you can make this room lighter, sir?"

I never realized how uncomfortable handcuffs are. The metal is digging into the bone of my hand.

"There is a button over there by the light switch at the door. Touch the top one, and the blinds will all open up."

Light fills the room immediately. My eyes aren't entirely adjusted, and it floods in quicker than my pupils can keep up. Both officers seem momentarily blinded as well, although the female doesn't squint as much as Officer Nick here.

"Do you have a license on you that we can run? I want to get this sorted out as quickly as possible, but we need to verify your identities."

"I am Grayson Sterling. I have a California driver's license in my wallet." I stand up and turn around, indicating that my wallet is in my back pocket. Officer Fat Fingers reaches in and pulls it out. If I weren't tied up like this, I might punch him. I guess that is why this procedure, the whole putting me in handcuffs thing, is necessary.

"I do not know that woman downstairs, and I want her arrested immediately."

"Sir, we aren't arresting anyone right now. We have officers downstairs talking to her like we are talking to you up here. We need to identify you first, and then we will get down to figuring out what is going on here."

"I hope you put her in handcuffs just like you did me," I huff. I am tired of this idea that women, somehow, aren't bad people. She will probably flaunt her obvious beauty, those full tits, and talk her way out of this. It is plain to see she can't be trusted, even if she does have a pretty face and a tight little body. Women always use that shit to get out of or into whatever they want.

"Handcuffs are standard operating procedure for any situation like this. I can assure you that she is getting the exact same treatment. Let's focus on you and your side of the story right now. Let the officers downstairs focus on her."

The female officer took my wallet and license downstairs. Why does she need my entire wallet to figure out that I am the rightful owner of this house? I will count every bill when I get it back. I have over a thousand dollars cash in there.

"I already told you. I own this house and have no idea who she is or why she is here. And her dog tried to maul me. That is all I got."

32

Finally, my breathing isn't so labored. My heart isn't beating out of my chest.

"Okay, slow down. You said you don't live here. When did you arrive? How long have you been here? Did you hear her come inside the residence, and if so, when? Why didn't you call 911?"

He has a pad out now and is recording my answers. None of this is rocket science. I own the damn house. She does not. A simple records search will confirm what I am saying.

"I flew into Norfolk this morning, drove here, and arrived around noon. I walked in and came straight upstairs via the elevator under the house. I accessed it using my key. I didn't see her then. But who knows, maybe she was lying in wait? I came in and went immediately to the bed to take a nap. I woke up to go to the bathroom probably ten or fifteen minutes ago, and that is when that animal tried to attack me. I didn't call 911 because my phone was on the bedside table over there." I nod my head towards the table on the opposite side of the bed.

"And then I stayed locked in that goddam bathroom for however long until you guys arrived."

"Okay, I need to stay put. I am going to go downstairs and speak with the officers down there to see what her story is. Office Jenecki will stay here with you. Hopefully it is a big misunderstanding and we can get it sorted out in no time.

SIX

Hollis

4:49 pm EST

"TAKE care of that sweet boy, will you?" Officer Creedmore, the female officer, says as she opens her patrol door, referring to Mr. Bojangles. He always has a way of defusing a tense situation.

"You know I will. He sure takes care of me. Thanks for your quick help today."

She gets into her car and looks back to me, "That is what we do. Glad it was all a misunderstanding."

Her door closes, and her engine starts. I kneel down and hug on Mr. Bojangles. I wonder if he is as exhausted as I am from all the excitement.

I wave goodbye to the last patrol car as it pulls out of the driveway. A sadness overtakes me. What am I sad about? That I'll never see Officer Creedmore again? Surely not. It is more likely because I am suddenly homeless.

Once we all realized there was some mix-up about me being able to rent this house and that it was just a giant misunderstanding, the cops wrote a report that we all had to sign. And that was it.

My first skirmish with the cops was rather underwhelming. I guess anything would have been underwhelming compared with the adrenaline apocalypse I experienced during those fifteen or so minutes between the first signs of life above me and their arrival.

I showed them my Airbnb confirmation email with this address listed, which also gave me access to the lockbox for access. I paid for the week to the tune of $6,500, so I am not leaving without a refund and some assurance that I can find another rental. Part of what I love about the Outer Banks is that it is remote and unknown. It's not like I can walk out of here today and find a new place to stay with the snap of my finger.

We are all perplexed as to how this was even up for rent on the site. The name on the Airbnb account was Claire Meyer, and the guy did say he knew her. At first, he denied it, but then his face turned a deep shade of purple when it looked like something clicked. After a moment, he declared that he was pretty sure he knew who was behind it. She must be someone he knows who has access to the house. An ex, perhaps?

Either way, we agreed to find an amicable solution and assured the cops we could do so without their help.

Now that Mr. Bojangles has calmed down, he's been wagging his tail over and over and begging for pets and rubs. He's stealing the show like he always does. I think the tension on both sides has been sufficiently eradicated.

Now, to figure out how to resolve this unfortunate situation. What a cluster. It's not something I want to deal with right now.

As I stand here on the front lawn, the mansion, for lack of better words, behind me, I take a breath. The sound is in front of me, tiny whitecaps floating by at a pretty fast clip. The brisk wind creates a bit of a ruffle on the usually calm water. I wrap my arms around myself, suddenly aware of the chill that has settled in the air.

The seagulls are in full effect, trying to tell me that everything will work out.

I have no idea who this Grayson man is, but he seems important. And he has a highly violent potty mouth. I will have to give him a little grace. Being awakened and almost attacked by a large dog in your own home would be frightening for anyone.

But boy, howdy, he is one hot piece of meat. I mean, he seems like an utterly pompous asshole, but a girl can still appreciate a square jaw and piercing blue eyes. My brain didn't register that at first, but as we sat in the kitchen, handcuffs removed, I really took him all in. And, whoa.

Okay, let's move on from that shallow observation. I need to come up with a plan for myself. I need this week. I just got here yesterday afternoon, and the thought of leaving, even if he gives me back my money and then some for my trouble, almost makes me cry.

Shit. I forgot to pick up my car. To compound things, I don't have a way to get anywhere too far until it opens again tomorrow morning.

I could use a good cry. I haven't cried over Bowen, which I find extremely unsettling. Maybe a good, ugly cry will clean out all of my clogged emotional pores so that my feelings can flow freely again.

I think I have an idea.

But first, Mr. Bojangles and I are going for a walk. I need to shake off this heavy weight on me. This sadness. The coming down from that adrenaline rush is deflating. Isn't that supposed to be invigorating, not depressing?

I don't bother going in to get the leash. Mr. B. will stay with me on the beach. I will be surprised if there are even any other walkers out there due to how windy it has gotten. The temperature has probably dropped ten degrees since we came back from lunch.

SEVEN

Grayson

5:12 pm EST

MY PHONE BUZZES in my back pocket. It's Olivier. His timing is impeccable. I am still reeling from the dumpster fire that just went down at my house. But I'm starting to put the pieces together regarding how this happened. Now, I need to look into a few things before I know for sure.

"Sterling," I answer my phone. I have no desire for pleasantries.

"Hello, Mr. Sterling. I just wanted to let you know that I have arrived in Duck, and I will be staying at the Sanderling Resort, as usual, in the event you need me before tomorrow morning. Is there anything you need tonight?"

I hadn't planned on having him available, but I feel my spirit lifting somewhat at the sound of this.

"I will be there at eight on the dot tomorrow morning for your trip to Virginia Beach if not."

"Thank you for the call, Olivier. If you are open and up for it, I would greatly appreciate it if you could drive me to dinner tonight at Cafe Pamlico." Olivier is very familiar with my favorite haunt when I am here.

"If not, no worries at all. There is a car here that I can use." I say this last part begrudgingly. Mainly because I have no desire to get back in that vehicle again. But I will if need be. I have to get out of here for a bit.

"It would be my pleasure, Sir. Do you have a time in mind?"

"How about 5:30?" That is quick and an extremely early dinner for me, but I need to figure all of this out, and I desperately need a glass of wine. His resort is a stone's throw from my house, so driving here will take him no more than two minutes.

"That works, Sir. I will see you then."

Click. There is no desire for long goodbyes, either.

Olivier has been driving for me all over the East Coast for nearly five years. If I tell him I will be in Manhattan on a specific date, he will be there with a Bentley. If I call him the following week and tell him I will be in Miami, he shows up with a Range Rover.

I don't ask how he can be in all the places at the drop of a hat, but I have a feeling it has something to do with how well I pay him. For these six days, for instance, he will make nearly $50,000 in addition to all expenses, including gas, lodging, and food.

If my memory serves me correctly, he made over $500,000 on my payroll in 2022. And I doubt I am his only client. Maybe his most lucrative, which gives me priority, I'm sure. All in all, we probably spend two months a year together.

Cafe Pamlico is one of my all-time favorite stomping grounds. I usually have dinner there every night when I am in town. I call it contemporary coastal with a dash of southern hospitality. The wine selection is perfection, the perfect complement to the fantastic food. I travel all over the world and eat at some of the most famous restaurants, but Cafe Pamlico wins every time.

One of the things I love is that if you're not looking for the place, you very well could miss it. It is tucked away, down a drive with thick hedges. It is my own little hidden oasis. Mine and two hundred people who also know about it. There is usually a line out the door to get a table.

The panorama visible from my favorite spot at the end of the bar is unparalleled. Expansive open views of the sound and the green marsh grass before it. Truly breathtaking.

I always order a bottle of their Silver Oak Cabernet Sauvignon. My mouth waters just thinking about it. If I'm being especially cheery, I get a second bottle. Steve, the owner, lets me take home what I don't finish. I do that to prolong the experience from the privacy of my own deck.

I start looking through my calendar to see the last time I was here at my beach house. I also pull up the surveillance footage to go through at high speed the previous six months. I never look at this stuff, leaving it to my security detail, but I make sure I have access.

Based on my calculations, people have stayed here almost consistently when I've been away. Somebody has been renting my house through a short-term rental service. Motherfucker.

And I am pretty sure I know who it is.

Claire Stackhouse. She is not my principal assistant, but she has been with me for two years, and I trust her with a lot of my personal stuff. Obviously, I trusted her too much. Technically, she is the executive assistant to my executive assistant, Everly. But she has her hands on pretty much all of my stuff.

Now, to figure out how she is running this little side hustle. I search Airbnb and VRBO for a high-end rental on or near Kill Devil Hills and Kitty Hawk. No one has ever heard of Duck, but anyone who knows anything about the Outer Banks or wants to visit, those are two of the islands at the top of the list of destinations to search for. My place is near to both of them.

There are many ocean-front and sound-front homes throughout the Outer Banks, but very few high-end homes like mine. If the house is listed for rent, it should be reasonably easy to spot. I set the rental price high to weed out the lower-end results.

Mother fucking bingo. Son of a bitch.

It is on Airbnb and listed for just over a grand a night. Underpriced amateurs. I'm sure she is making a fortune on this. With no expenses except for a cleaning after each guest, this might be the most innovative business venture ever. Except that she is essentially stealing it from me.

I'm all about ingenuity and finding an angle, especially in real estate. But this is a bridge too far. Perhaps Claire doesn't know me well enough. With practically any of my other homes, I might not have the reaction I am having inside of me right now. Hell, there is a good chance I never would have even found out. But this place is my sacred place. My hideaway. And she just shat all over it, letting strangers stay in my bed, use my things.

I am seething. Everly is out of town on vacation right now, but this demands her attention. If I find out she was in on this in any way, not only will I fire her ass, but I will have both of them arrested.

On second thought, I am not going to call Everly. I made a promise to her, unsolicited, that I would not interrupt her vacation. She works hard for me, and when she is off, she deserves it. Anyway, I need to find out if she is involved first.

I text Andrew Bartles, my private investigator. He is headquartered in Fort Worth, but he can do better and faster research on pretty much any person or business than anyone I've ever worked with. And if I need boots on the ground, no matter where it is, he is always ready to travel.

We have worked together since my early days in L.A. I trust him with my life, literally. He specializes in C-Suite and executive-level clients. He knows how to find out things that most people think are only thoughts in their own heads. He is that good.

> Andrew, I apologize for the late text. I have an emergency I need you to take care of for me if you're still on the clock.

Andrew works tirelessly and ceaselessly. I already know he will acquiesce. Unless he is in a bunker with no service. I don't see how that hot wife of his puts up with his shit. But it works for me.

> Sure, boss. What's up?

Just like I thought.

> Can you look into 3 N Baum Trail, Duck, NC 27949, for me? I need to know everything you can find on it as a short-term or vacation rental. I want to know how often it has been rented in the last ten years, how much income it has generated, and a list of any guests you can find. And whose name and contact information are on the rental.

Sure, Boss. This is your place on the Outer Banks, right? I didn't realize you were renting it.

> Yes, it is. And I haven't been. That is why I need you to get me everything you can find. Someone has been renting it, and I need to know who.

I'm on it. Be in touch soon.

I rack my brain for a solution to the current problem. The studio under the house is being renovated. A few months ago, there was an undetected leak, and the whole apartment had to be gutted. So that is out.

I also own a small cottage on the sound side a few miles away. I purchased it for the project manager I hired from Las Vegas to stay in while this house was being built years ago. I held onto it because it was such a sweet little house on over two acres. I have rented it out long-term ever since. It will be vacant in just a few weeks, but that doesn't do anyone any good right now.

I hit my forehead with the thumb side of my closed fist. "Come on," I say to myself. I can think of a solution to this debacle. I've had more complex puzzles to solve.

I pick up my phone and search for The Sanderling Resort.

"It's a great evening at the Sanderling. How can I assist you?"

"Hi, I was calling to see if you have any rooms available for the next week?"

After a brief hold, she returns, "I'm sorry, we are booked for this weekend, but I could get you something as soon as Monday. Will that work?"

Irritated again, I reply in my kindest voice, "No, I don't think that will. I will call back if so. Thank you."

I hang up the phone and toss it onto the table.

I suppose I can stay in the apartment under the house. I can rough it for a few days. As much as I want to offer it to her, I don't feel right even proposing that to her. This lady, even though her dog could have killed me today, doesn't deserve to be kicked out of what she paid for or asked to stay in the half-completed basement apartment.

I have to be here for work until Tuesday. This house is almost ten thousand square feet. Surely we can make it work.

EIGHT

Hollis

5:22 pm EST

THE SUN IS SETTING, the sky a soft mix of purple and pink, and the coolness is still growing. I would venture to say it is straight-up cold now. The wind is still really moving, and without the sun to contrast it, the nip is real.

If I didn't know any better, I would not think it is spring and that it was over seventy degrees yesterday.

I don't feel comfortable coming into the house from the beachside, so we pass it at the end of our walk. It feels strange for me to walk up the deck stairs that lead directly to the beach of what now feels like someone else's home. Just a few hours ago, it felt like mine. Now that has been spoiled, and I feel like I am the intruder.

There is a beach access about five houses down. I walk through there and to the street. The sand on the dune is fine and soft, contradicting the harder, wet sand on the beach near the waves. The soles of my feet enjoy the contrasting sensations. The cool silk sends a shiver through me.

I throw down my flip-flops to put them back on. The sand caught between my feet and the flip-flop serves as the exfoliant that I so desperately need. It's not as relaxing as a pedicure, but it will do.

I walk down the street, backtracking to the house. Once I reach it, I take a deep breath and ready myself for the unknown. This man has not been warm or kind in any way, so I don't foresee anything different. My insides tense at the prospect of dealing with him.

The truth is, though, I will be fine not getting any refund if we can work out a solution that allows me to stay here through next week, as I planned. I don't have another house to go to right now, and I really need to figure out my life moving forward. I don't have the mental capacity to go there yet. I was counting on this reset to give me the clarity I need for where I go from here.

It's ironic and sort of hilarious. I planned and paid for this house two months in advance, but I still have no idea where I will live in five days after I leave here.

I'm sure it is part denial and part indifference. I was looking forward to a quiet, uneventful week at the beach. That, I presumed, would open the floodgates for my vision of where I needed to be for this next chapter of my life.

Bowen and I had gotten so good at avoiding each other once we decided to divorce that living in the same house but apart was no stretch. He just no longer called the primary bedroom his. That became my room, and he took up residence in the guest room across the hall.

I didn't think we could possibly see each other less. But once we started the divorce talk, a week could sometimes pass without me even seeing him, much less interacting with him.

Without a specific conversation to do so, I believe we both just chartered our movements to avoid each other. If we didn't see each other, there was no awkwardness to smooth out.

Now, the primary bedroom is probably back to being his. And I am essentially homeless. I am sure if I called him and needed a place to crash, he would be fine with it. But I will literally live in a box under a bridge before doing that.

I knock on the front door. Mr. Bojangles sits at my feet, blissfully unaware of the angst and awkwardness of this situation. He looks up at me as if I am crazy. He is probably wondering why we aren't just walking in like we have been for the last twenty-four hours.

No answer. I knock again.

This passive-aggressive man better not be ignoring me on purpose. I try the doorknob to see if it is locked. Cold brass fills my fist. I turn it lightly, checking to see if it is locked.

Maybe I was too naive, thinking we would work this out like two adults. I should have insisted on a solution with the cops present, as they suggested.

All of my stuff, not that I have a lot, but everything in this world that belongs to me is inside that house. And I didn't think to bring a key with me when I walked out to take a stroll on the beach. I just assumed we both could use a break. Now, I am probably out of luck. Again.

The brass door knob turns entirely, and there is a clicking sound as the latching mechanism releases. The heavy door opens without any force by me. Gravity invites me in.

I stick only my head in, holding Mr. Bojangles back with my foot.

"Hello. Grayson? Anyone home? It's me, Hollis Mitchell. Hellooooo?"

Mr. Bojangles sits down again at my feet and looks up at me again. Now he really thinks I have lost it. Like, what are you doing, lady?

I push through and walk in. There is a note on the side entry table to the right and a single key on a key ring.

> Ms. Mitchell,
>
> I know you paid good money to stay here and will unlikely find another place on short notice. It's not your fault that someone did something underhanded. You are welcome to stay here for the time you thought you rented the house as long as you don't mind that I will be coming and going until Tuesday. I will be going to Virginia every day so that you will have the place to yourself. I will stay in the studio apartment. I will also be refunding the entire amount you paid.
>
> If this is agreeable to you, please text me at 213-566-4663 and let me know. I've gone into town and will be back late.

Grayson Sterling

Well, butter my butt and call me a biscuit. That was completely unexpected. All of it. Reasonableness. Empathy. Generosity. Deference.

I am blown away. I take a seat in the navy blue velvet armchair beside the entry table. The marble-topped table is cold to the touch, even through my sweatshirt. I look back at the note and reread it.

I let my hand fall to my lap, still clutching the note between my fingers. This is better than I could have hoped for. Am I crazy for wanting to share a house with a stranger? What other options do I have? I lean my head back in the chair and sit with it for a moment. Mr. Bojangles rests his head on my knee.

My mind is churning—so many questions. I feel presumptuous taking him up on this. I stay in the house, and he stays in the studio apartment instead of his own home?

He won't be back until late? What does this guy do? He has this amazing place and seems to spend his time everywhere but here. If this were mine, it would be hard to get me to leave.

I need a bath. My head is pounding from all of the excitement earlier. My back and legs are killing me.

And you know what? I'm going to take him up on his offer. No one ever does for me. I constantly bend backward for others, never wanting to put anyone out. My therapist says I need to let others do for me every once in a while. I don't know this guy from Adam, so why not?

And he almost killed my dog. So yes, I am staying in the primary bedroom. I pick up my phone and shoot him a text.

> Thank you for your generous offer. I will take you up on it because I do not know where I would go otherwise. Please don't feel banished to the apartment unless you prefer a separate space. This house is plenty big enough for the two of us. I will make sure to stay out of your hair when you are home. I'm surprisingly adept at doing that. I am scheduled to leave on Wednesday. - Hollis Mitchell

NINE

Grayson

Cafe Pamlico

8:49 PM *EST*

IT'S ALMOST NINE, and I am staring out of the large plate glass window at a Blue Heron walking gracefully along the marsh edge when texts from Andrew Bartles start coming in.

Hey, Boss. I just emailed a bunch of stuff to you that I found on your house in the OB. Claire Meyer, aka Claire Stackhouse, and Curtis Meyer are the two names that show up on all of the STR applications, rental sites, and contact forms for rent requests. In the last twelve months, it has been rented for a total of 226 days for a total income before expenses of $251,684. It was taken down yesterday, but some ghost listings are still available to see on both VRBO and Airbnb. So, while the calendar shows no availability, I can see that the listing was removed. Sometimes, the STR sites will continue to list it to capture people looking—sort of a bait-and-switch tactic.

Son of a bitch.

Thank you, Andrew. Did you double-check to make sure there is no mention or connection to Everly Stern or Jacob Stern? I need to know specifically if there is any connection there. Thanks for your hard and always quick work.

It appears on the surface that Everly wasn't involved in this scheme, but I need to ask specifically to be sure. Before releasing my hellfire on this, I want to know every single detail.

Nope. Not a thing. There are three emails associated with any and every piece I could find concerning the STR: stayintheOBX@gmail.com, stackthehouse@gmail.com, and meyerck@me.com. All three email addresses were created and managed from an IP address that is associated with Curtis Meyer. The physical address is the one in the email I sent in Anaheim, and Claire Meyer filled out the STR application.

Thanks for taking the time to dig into this. I really needed to know what was going on and fast. You always come through.

I know I said I would be out late, but my eyes are begging for sleep. I feel confident we are both adults here, and now that we have discussed it, if only by the written word, I don't think it is inappropriate for me to come back and go straight to bed.

Olivier: I am ready to head back to the house. I have asked for the check, so I should be ready to go in the next ten minutes or so. Thanks!

Teddy brings my check and takes my credit card with a smile. He must see that I am not in the mood for small talk.

The restaurant is full. Everyone appears jovial and thrilled to have gotten a coveted seat in this sacred space. I'm not taking up much space in my 2-seater booth, but I am sure they will have it cleaned up and filled with a googly-eyed couple within minutes of me leaving.

The night is clear. The sky is a deep periwinkle, the almost full moon giving off enough light to see the greens and yellows on the marsh grass from here. The ripples on the water are still moving at a good speed, telling me the wind is still kicking.

I gulp the last of the wine in my glass just as Teddy brings me back my Mastercard Black, the slip to sign, and my second bottle of wine in a wine carrier.

"Thank you so much for joining us again, Mr. Sterling. I hope you enjoyed your evening. Will you be here in the Outer Banks for a while?"

"Thank you, Teddy. I will be here through next week, but I'll be traveling to Virginia during the day for work. I am not sure when, but I know I will be back at least one more time before I head back to the West Coast. Thanks for taking care of me. I appreciate it."

"I do hope to see you again. Have a great rest of the night."

> Ms. Mitchell: I just wanted to let you know I am heading back that way. I didn't want to alarm you, and I hope to avoid being attacked by your dog. I will take you up on the offer to stay in the main house because the apartment is currently in disarray. You won't even know I am there. Thank you.

———

9:27 PM *EST*

I STEP out of the shower and towel off my wet hair. Oddly enough, I have never showered in this bathroom after owning this house for almost ten years. This house was built with four bedroom suites on the main floor, in addition to mine on the second floor that I use.

Even though I never became an architect, I remember some things my grandfather said and try to implement where I can. And when I design a residence, I make each bedroom a complete suite, especially when it comes to vacation homes.

According to my grandfather, a house with only one primary bedroom is a dead giveaway that someone didn't have enough money to build a home properly. Ideally, every room needs its own restroom and an ingress/egress.

Thank goodness this suite has a door leading outside to the large beach deck.

I bought this land in 2009 when the real estate market was still in freefall. Many people thought I was crazy. I could sell the land alone now for four times what I paid for it then, not even considering the several million dollar residence on it. It took over a year to design the perfect house for this spot and almost two years to build it.

I have been so tired all day, and now, with my shower and my belly full, I can't believe I am not falling into the bed immediately to sleep. I need a nightcap and one more look at the deep blue sky and big, bright moon.

I wonder if that woman is awake. I would need to go into the kitchen to get a wine opener and a glass. Mental note: make sure each room has a wet bar complete with wine glasses and an opener.

What am I worrying about?! This is my house, and I already told her I would refund her. It isn't like I am going to go through her panties drawer. And that damn dog better be tied up.

I crack the door and listen for any signs of life out there. The air is clear—only some soft lights from the automatic lamps that come on and stay on at night. I walk to the wet bar and grab what I need, grateful there is no interruption. I shake my head that I am pussyfooting in my own house, worried I might disrupt a stranger. Anger rises again to the forefront of my thoughts that I am even in this predicament.

I open the heavy sliding glass door that heads out to the ocean. The wind finally calmed down, leaving the cool, crisp, refreshing air behind. I pour a glass of wine and set the bottle on the side table. Finally, peace and quiet. I can enjoy my favorite strip of land on this earth.

TEN

Hollis

9:42 pm EST

I HEAR Grayson sit down in the teak chair on the other end of the deck. Then, the base of his wine glass clinks as it hits the hard wood on the arm of the chair. I am frozen and not sure how to handle this situation. Mr. Bojangles puts his head up, stirred from his slumber. He is immediately aware that someone else is here. Thank goodness he doesn't make a scene like earlier.

I would slink off and head upstairs, leaving him to the entire deck. But then he would be aware of my presence. And that would be awkward. If I can stay still and Mr. B doesn't try to attack him, then we can coexist out here until he goes back in, and he will be none the wiser. He doesn't seem the type to sit still for long, so maybe this will be a quick trip out to check the waves and then back in.

The clean smells of soap and aftershave waft over to me. Those smells get me every time. Even Bowen smelled delicious when he came to bed fresh from the shower. I'm a little weird. The strangest things turn me on.

Mr. Bojangles scratches his neck with his hind leg, jingling the metal tags on his collar. So much for being incognito until Mr. Fickle goes back inside.

"Motherfucker! You scared the shit out of me. I had no idea you were there."

Watch your mouth, I want to say. How does someone get through life talking like that?

"Sorry, I guess I fell asleep on the hammock. We will go inside. Sorry." I fumble, looking like a complete idiot caught in a spider web, unable to escape.

I lie. I've totally been awake the whole time. I heard him come in. I saw the light in his room come on, offering a soft glow on the deck from the big glass window sliding glass door. I heard the shower come on and then go off. I've been here for the whole routine.

"No, it's okay. It's a big deck. I think we can both be out there. As long as your dog doesn't try to take a chunk out of my leg."

"Oh, Mr. Bojangles is a big teddy bear. I don't know what got into him today, but he wouldn't hurt a flea."

"Did you really name your dog 'Mr. Bojangles?'"

With that, he lets out a big, genuine laugh. We get that reaction a lot. I'm glad to know this guy has a sense of humor, though.

"It's a long story, but my husband loved this skit on Saturday Night Live about two dogs named Rocky Balboa and Mr. Bojangles."

My dog's name is always a good icebreaker. A segue out of awkward moments. He is a protector in more ways than one.

"Ex," I correct myself.

"Pardon me?

"Ex-husband. I said husband, I meant ex-husband."

This is going to take some getting used to. So strange. We have been estranged for so long, so it should be easy. Right? For some reason, it leaves a lump in my throat, though.

"Oh. Gotcha. That's quite the name."

I let out a little fake laugh. I don't know what else to do or say. So much for smoothing over the awkwardness.

"Would you like a glass of wine?" he asks. "It's the best Pinot Noir I've ever had. I have a whole bottle here."

Is he extending an olive branch here? I'm not much of a wine drinker, but it would be rude not to accept his attempt to make nice after our calamitous introduction a few hours ago.

"I was about to go in to get another hot tea. Would you mind if I do that and then join you?"

Is that too forward? I'm not trying to buddy up to him, but I could use a refresher. And if we are going to be living together, per se, I might as well know who I'm sharing a roof with.

"That would be nice, as a matter of fact. Yes, please do join me."

I dare say he is somewhat amenable. Like Mr. Bojangles, his bark and growl betrayed the nice guy underneath. He said several words without a single curse word.

I make the difficult job of getting out of the hammock look even more ungraceful than it is normally, if that is even possible. I'm trying not to step on Mr. Bojangles while also ensuring I am centered so I don't fall over. I have been lying here for a while, so my legs are a little wobbly.

"Can I get you anything while I am inside?"

This is strange, offering to get something for him from his own house.

"No, thank you."

A man of few words. This little meeting on the ocean-front deck will be short. Or painfully long. But I need to be a hospitable guest. Or host. Or whatever it is that I am in this strange arrangement.

I return with my chai tea, my hands wrapped around the hot porcelain mug. It feels good, warming my whole body. A comforting ritual I have grown to love at night. The cinnamon and cloves are climbing up to my nose, filling me with the most delicious, warm hug.

I take a seat beside him in the matching oversized wood chair. My body sinks down deep, more than I realized it would. It is quite deep, and I almost spill my hot tea on my lap.

His handsomeness strikes me again. His chestnut hair is wavy and looser than it was this morning. He has a little more stubble than he did earlier, too. His facial hair is clearly thick and proliferates. It has only been a few hours since I last saw him, and his face was as smooth as a baby's bottom then.

"It's a beautiful night. I haven't interacted with anyone since I woke up to a shitty alarm at five this morning except for work, so it is nice to spend time with a person I am not paying to talk to me."

"Well, technically, you are paying me. Remember, you are refunding what I paid to rent."

I'm trying to be funny, but that came out all wrong. As soon as I say it, I want to punch myself in the stomach. Stupid. Stupid.

"Ha! You're right. Well, thanks for joining me anyway."

"In all seriousness, I do appreciate you honoring my reservation. Do you mind me asking what happened here? If you don't want to talk about it, I understand. It has all been just a little bit jarring. And this is all really quite unconventional. I can't imagine having my home rented out without my knowledge."

"I don't really want to go into that bullshit right now if it is okay with you. However, an employee listed and managed my personal home on the short-term rental site without my permission or knowledge. I am handling it."

Eeek. That is quite bold of said employee. And a sticky situation for sure. This guy is so warm and sharing.

Not.

I'm wondering why he invited me to join him. Perhaps he just meant a warm body, no conversation.

I take a big slurp of my tea. When enjoying my tea, I am usually more civilized, especially around strangers. But it is hot, and I am trying not to burn my tongue again. Plus, I couldn't care less what this jerk thinks about me. Even if he is hotter than the sun.

ELEVEN

Grayson

9:59 pm EST

I AM NOT sure why I insisted on her joining me. I must have had a momentary lapse of my better judgment. Her slurping is entirely annoying. But there is also something very refreshing and engaging about this woman at the same time.

She smells amazing, for one thing. It's a rich and floral scent but not too sweet. I'm intrigued and want to dig in more.

"So, are you from around here?" I ask. Maybe she is one of these fisher-people I admire from afar.

"Sort of, but not really. I mean, I am not from here here, but I have been visiting most of my life."

"Hmmm." More. Give me more, lady. Trying to be mysterious, I see.

"How long have you owned this house?" She asks. "It is quite amazing, as I'm sure you are aware. This stretch of the beach is so quiet, it almost feels private," she says, steering the conversation.

"Thank you. I bought the property a while back and built the house almost ten years ago. I do love it here. My permanent residence is on the West Coast. Where are you from?"

"I've been coming to the Outer Banks since I was a kid. I've never owned anything here, but I still consider this my second home."

She doesn't quite answer the question entirely. Is that on purpose, or am I extrapolating too much from what she is not saying? She also looks pretty familiar with my home, and it occurs to me that this isn't the first time she has stayed here.

"Have you rented my house before?" I ask.

"Oh, no. I couldn't normally afford this rate. I just needed a special treat, and when I came across your place, I had to splurge."

She is going on and on about the Outer Banks and the different little fishing towns up and down the barrier islands. She does know the island and seems very passionate about it. This touches me because I feel the same. I am not as well-versed as she is about the area, but this stretch of the eastern coastline holds an extraordinary place in my heart.

"This property came on my radar because of the relatively inexpensive price for ocean-front property. I purchased a hundred acres of unspoiled waterfront for next to nothing back in 2009. And when I came here to research and draft a development plan, I fell in love. That is why I never capitalized on it by developing it. It might be one of the last unspoiled paradises in the US."

"You planned to develop this property?"

"Yes. The town of Duck has only existed on a registry in this state since 1985. In fact, The Sanderling Resort, just a few miles up, opened that year and put this stretch of sand on the map. Before that, it was just a long swathe of an overgrown dune against the Atlantic Ocean. When I saw the opportunity for what it was, I jumped on the land. But now I want to keep it all to myself."

We both sit on that notion for a moment. The thought of this oasis we both apparently care deeply about turned into a busy, traffic-ridden tourist trap is an ugly one.

"Or, at least, I thought I wanted to keep it to myself until someone decided to rent out my home unbeknownst to me," I add.

"I'm very sorry someone betrayed your trust like that."

The way she says that makes me sure she is sincere. And it feels good. Sometimes, I just want to feel like someone sees me as a person at the end of the day.

"And I can say that I am glad it fell into your hands and not into those of someone else who would surely have turned it into the next Myrtle Beach. I just don't know what I will do if this town is ever developed like that. The lack of development is one of the things that makes this place so special."

"Over the years, I have purchased property here and there along the North Carolina coast. I own more property than any other single person in all of the Outer Banks. And I don't plan to ever develop. So as long as I have a say, this will never become the next tourist beach attraction."

"You are my twin flame, then. I owe you my gratitude, Sir," she says with an easy, engaging smile.

As I pour the last of my wine from the bottle, I feel a sadness that I haven't felt in a long time. A stark realization hits me: I am enjoying this unconventional evening with a complete stranger. I feel no pressure or anger. I am not annoyed for the first time since waking up this morning.

I also feel a burning inside of me that I haven't felt in I don't know how long. I was with a woman a few months ago. A friend set me up with her. Everyone seems so concerned that I'm closing in on my mid-thirties, and I am not married yet.

I am perfectly happy running my business, building and growing. That is my focus and how I enjoy spending my time. But that doesn't stop countless people from trying to solve a problem that doesn't exist and playing matchmaker.

She and I got along fine, but there was absolutely nothing in it for me. We went to dinner a few times and had a handful of encounters. Besides the sex, I had no desire for things to go anywhere with her. According to our mutual friend, she felt differently, but it just wasn't there for me. So I ended it, not wanting to hurt her or our mutual friends.

In contrast, I am finding myself mesmerized by this woman. She is warm and engaging. Refreshing. Most of the women I meet organically, either through business or out with friends, are completely consumed with how they look and how much money their next prospective date makes. Hollis couldn't seem to care less about either of those things. And her natural beauty leaps out from under her hoodie.

We are approaching midnight. It appears we both are enjoying each other's banter. The wind is nonexistent, and the temperature has dropped even further. Suddenly, I'm feeling a little cold. I know she must be, too. But I'm not ready for the night to end.

"Hollis, Would you like to continue the conversation inside? We can start the gas logs in the living room, and you can get a refresher on your tea. I notice your teeth are chattering a bit, and quite honestly, I'm chilly now, too."

Her head is nodding before I even get the last words out.

"That sounds great. I have been getting too much rest, sleeping in and taking naps. I enjoy learning more about you, the development business, and the West Coast. These are all so foreign to me, and it's fascinating."

At that very moment, our eyes meet. An electric current surges through my veins, igniting something within me. Her smile casts warmth and joy, captivating me. The way she carries herself with confidence and grace is magnetic. Either I am delirious, or she is drawing me in. Perhaps both.

Her intelligence and wit leave me wanting more as we continue to talk. I find myself hanging onto every word that comes out of her delicious lips. It's as if we share an unspoken connection, a deep understanding that transcends words. Her presence fills the air with a new type of energy I've never encountered.

We both get up and head in. The giant red dog follows closely behind her. He is growing on me, too.

TWELVE

Hollis
___

10:57 pm EST

I AM CHILLED to the bone. My tea has been finished for close to an hour and I only have a hoodie on over my t-shirt. But I have enjoyed the conversation so much that I muscled through the freeze.

I didn't realize how hungry I have been for male companionship. Even if he is a little brooding and has a potty mouth. I see the smile peeking through his gruff and curt exterior.

He is interesting. And I like the fact that even though he has enough money to do whatever he wants, he cares about the North Carolina coastline so much that he won't exploit it.

As we walk inside, I can't help but obsess over his toned physique. He is tall, fit, and very handsome. His tight little butt moving as he takes each step makes me imagine it perfectly with no clothes on. I am awe-struck. His Vuori joggers hug him in just the right places. I have to make myself look up before he turns around and busts me staring.

I head straight to the kitchen to turn on my electric kettle, which I always carry with me when traveling. It boils water in less than a minute. I wash out my mug, pour the loose tea into my French press, and prepare it for my water. I love the whole ritual of making tea. I go for the Chamomile this time. No caffeine after midnight makes sense.

My hulking hero is in the living room getting the fire started. Okay, I might be getting ahead of myself, but imagining a beautiful hunk of meat here in this romantic place is fun, getting the fire ready for a late-night snuggle in front of the wide-open ocean. A girl can dream.

"You said you own a lot of property around here. Do you, by chance, happen to own a less mansion-ish house near here that you wouldn't mind renting out long-term?"

This is more of a way for me to make conversation than a serious question, but I figure it can't hurt. I may be opening Pandora's Box here by asking, as I have clearly been avoiding telling him where I live since I don't actually live anywhere currently.

"As it turns out, I have gotten out of residential investments, but I did hold onto a little cottage here in Duck. I bought it years ago after I bought this property. It has been rented for the last six years to an older lady. She is moving to Charlotte at the end of this month to live with her daughter. Are you looking for a rental?"

What, are you freaking kidding me? Is this fate unfolding right here in front of me in real-time?

"Well, I am looking for something. Tell me more."

————

FRIDAY, *March 8*

12:59 am EST

I CAN'T BELIEVE we are still up talking. I've refilled my tea a second time and peed at least fifty times. Grayson is opening up like a tidal wave. He is extremely engaging. To the point that I could sit here and stare all night into his blue eyes. Eyes that look like they had been dug out of the Atlantic Ocean and plopped into his face.

He has even lightened up on the curse words.

He is nothing like the first impression I had of him. Or, of the second, for that matter, when we were all sitting with the cops after they had removed both of our handcuffs. He was gruff and short on words, except for the eff word. Now, he is effusive, light, and totally engaging.

His wavy, messy hair is begging my hands to run my fingers through it. I am seriously questioning my own sanity. Why am I over here imagining running my hands over his chest when I haven't even known the man for twenty-four hours? When he pulled his quarter zip sweater over his head earlier, I had an uninterrupted, direct opportunity to study his supple skin and body for a good two seconds, and I willed time to stand still.

The fire is still crackling, and his eyes are still smiling at me. Mr. Bojangles is long out, not worried about me at all. I feel like I have quite literally struck gold here – I'm staying in this fabulous house on the beach, for free, with this billionaire Greek God. And now he tells me he has a rental coming up down the street.

"I'm serious about the house. I can leave the address for you to take a walk or bike ride over there tomorrow to check it out from the outside. Mrs. Zeddleman is still there, so I can't say you should knock, but if she is in the yard, feel free to introduce yourself. She is kind and easy."

"You have no idea what this would mean to me. I think it sounds perfect. Unless it is falling in on itself or has a tree growing up through the middle, I am pretty certain I will take it."

Now, to figure out what to do for the two or so weeks between here and there.

"Mr. Bojangles and I should probably call it a night. I have more tea in me than a British aristocrat. I've enjoyed our chat and am grateful that you allowed us to continue staying here."

If I am being honest, I don't want the night to end. But I feel like I am over-extending my welcome here.

"You're right. I have to be up again in just a few hours. The night sure got away from us. Thank you for spending your evening talking. I really enjoyed it, as well. I will leave the address for the cottage for you on the counter when I leave. I am not sure how early you are up and about, but my driver will be here, and I will be out by eight. Help yourself, of course, to whatever you need and make yourself at home."

My heart is melting right now. This man is kind. I had him completely wrong.

Does it make me a weirdo that I want to bury my nose in the nape of his neck? And those beautiful, piercing eyes. That unbelievable square jaw. Dear God, that is a beautiful man.

Mostly, though, the adult male conversation is what got me. It wasn't pulling teeth, as I have found it to be with most men. He was engaged and engaging. I was genuinely interested in what he had to say.

I can't remember, honestly, the last time Bowen and I sat and talked for hours. Maybe never.

The fact that Grayson has a rental here on the island that just happens to be coming available almost feels like fate. Kismet.

Here I am, due to some underhanded business by one of his employees, it seems, staying in his home. And I had no idea where I was going to live after my vacation was over. Like some modern-day Prince Charming, he appears with a solution to my problems.

"Thanks again. Sleep tight."

I open the front door to let Mr. Bojangles take a potty break. I really just wanted a breath of fresh air to organize all of this in my head. I have a strange stirring in my belly.

I shake my head. Between my lack of sleep and the tea overdose, my brain is having crazy thoughts. There nothing romantic going on here with him. I need to put it out of my head immediately. This man is letting me crash in his home, in his primary bedroom, for the week. And he will likely be my next landlord. End of story.

Get a hold of yourself, Hollis. This isn't a Disney movie. I may be a damsel in distress, but he is not my knight in shining armor.

"Hurry, Mr. Bojangles! It is cold!"

Mr. B. comes bounding up the steps, and we walk in. I lock the deadbolt and hang his leash on the arm of the chair. I remember that I left my water on the side table in the living room and turn back to get it for bed.

Looking down at my phone, I head towards the stairs. I am startled when I almost run into Grayson.

"Goodness! I am so sorry! I didn't know you were there."

I can feel something different than before I walked outside to take Mr. Bojangles to relieve himself. An energy I can't explain. I felt myself drawn to him before, but it seemed one-sided. Now, it feels mutual.

The burning deep inside of me warms every inch of my body. A tingling rises up and catches in my throat. Grayson doesn't say a word as he puts his hand behind my head and pulls me to him. His lips are suddenly on mine. I let go of any restraint I may have been holding onto and kiss him back.

THIRTEEN

Grayson

1:09 am EST

THE IRRESISTIBLE PULL within me has become too big to reel in any longer. A desire that I know is as illicit as it is undeniable takes hold. Logic tells me this will never develop into anything more and that I shouldn't allow myself to go there. But an inexplicable force magnetizes me to her.

She's a unique anomaly in my world. Nothing like the women I know. I am not interested in them, nor am I drawn to them. She is different somehow. Her aura and natural beauty set her apart from the rest.

Her authenticity, her inherent beauty, it all casts a spell on me. Our shared love for this tranquil stretch of the Atlantic coastline unites our completely different worlds into this harmonious moment.

The scent of the burning wood mixes with her inebriating perfume. A siren call.

She kisses me back. There is no resistance on either of our parts. I am bold and hungry for more of her. I lift her shirt over her head, exposing her full breasts. She isn't wearing anything under her thin t-shirt. Her soft, dewy skin is bare under the bulky hoodie, revealing a body that shouldn't stay hidden.

I run my hands along her raised arms, down her side, taking in every inch of her. I kiss her neck as she tilts her head back, inviting me in for more.

The heat from the fire mirrors the heat between us, intensifying the desire that courses through my veins. Our fingers meet, and I pull her closer, feeling the warmth of her nude skin against my chest through my shirt.

I need her closer to me.

I rip off my shirt, bringing her bare touch to mine. The feeling is indescribable. Invigorating. Intoxicating.

I pick her up and carry her down the hall to the room I am staying in. She can't weigh more than a hundred pounds soaking wet. I realize that I have a deep desire to want to protect her. Her legs are wrapped tightly around my waist, pulling her midsection closer to me. I can feel her wetness through her pants on me.

We walk into the room, and the air is noticeably cooler. The fire in the living room heated up more than my libido.

I place her on the bed, my forearms caught underneath the weight of her body. I slide them out to continue undressing.

I pull down my pants and my briefs, completely exposed before her, as she lays on the bed looking up at me. The lights are off, but a soft glow comes in from the hall. Her features are even more beautiful than I remember, highlighted at the perfect spots: her high cheekbones, her full lips.

I bend down and grab onto the top of her leggings. I slowly and sensually pull them down, following the trajectory with my mouth. My scruffy chin brushes her thigh and then her leg down to her feet as I pull the pants completely off. I kiss her legs every few inches as I get to know all of her.

It's a shame that the cold air kept all this under wraps. I fell under her spell with conversation, but now, seeing her body, I am utterly obsessed with her.

Every second is an eternity, and I am drinking her in— each beautiful, unspoiled inch of her. I run my fingers over her, lightly brushing her leg as I make my way back up to her. As I trail up her leg, my fingers find their way to the inside of her thighs. The skin is soft and warm. Goosebumps immediately emerge on her skin.

I climb onto her, lost in the moment's enthusiasm, and find my way inside her. She receives me as if we belong together. My parts fit with hers as if we were a puzzle coming together. I have to fight my body's urge to come right away, not wanting this moment to end. Every single nerve ending is on fire.

Her wet and warm and tight cavern squeezing my cock feels like an ecstasy I have never known. My entire body feels like it has entered into a new dimension.

She pulls her legs up behind me, allowing for me to thrust deeper into her. Each push feels like we are closer to becoming one. I savor each drive, sinking into her, wanting more and more. Nothing is ever enough.

She pushes me back, turning me over. She sits on top of me, and her hands brush my chest as she arches her back and yells out. I almost come with her but resist again, confident we still have more to do. She calls out my name, and I feel her tighten again on my cock.

She folds on top of me, continuing to gyrate, sliding up and down. I can tell she is spent, but she isn't stopping. Her back is wet with perspiration.

We flip back onto her back, and I step off of the bed, pulling her down to meet me. I continue my motion, in and out, lost in her. She is wet and swollen, eager for me.

In this moment, there is nothing else that exists. It's just the two of us, consumed by the intensity of our connection, engrossed in only each other.

I cannot hold it back any longer. I groan and start to pull out, and she stops me.

"I cannot get pregnant. Don't stop. Come inside of me."

I take one final thrust, deep and hard, leaving it in her. I explode. A climax like I have never experienced.

I pull myself out of her and climb beside her on the bed. I hold her, threading my arm under her neck, allowing her head to rest on my chest. We lay like that for I don't know how long.

Until I wake in the night and we are both naked, laying on top of the covers. I reach above her and pull the down comforter beneath her. I whisper to her, "Get in." She never opens her eyes but obliges, pulling the covers over herself and turning into me.

Her hand finds its way to my shaft, and she starts stroking me. It only takes two rubs of her hand on my sleepy cock, and it is fully engorged, awake, and hungry for her.

I climb on top of her, pull her legs up, and enter her. She was fast asleep only moments ago, but as I push myself into her, I feel how wet and ready she is for me. I almost lose it.

"Grayson, yes. You feel so good. Don't stop. Ohhhh…!"

I scream out with her. The slapping sound of our bodies hitting each other is the only noise, along with our groans in the otherwise deadly silent room.

My rhythm picks up, my cock so hard as it goes in and out. She pulls at my ass, pulling me deeper, harder into her.

We both climax together at the same time. I fall onto her, burying my head in her full breasts. I can hear her heart beating in her chest. I am aware of it slowly slowing, the thumps growing less fierce against her rib cage, growing quieter.

Her breathing calms. Neither of us says another word. We lay together like this. Her hand eventually stops brushing my back, resting on me.

The world goes black as I slide into a deep sleep.

FOURTEEN

Hollis

5:44 am EST

AS I SLOWLY OPEN MY eyes, the drowsiness begins to fade away. The early morning light shifts through tiny slivers on the sides of the blackout curtains. It barely reveals the unfamiliar surroundings of a bedroom I only peeked in before last night. It must be close to six in the morning.

The filtered, still-dark sky is lightening by the minute. Little by little, more sunlight breaks through, highlighting the space around me. Shadows are shifting, making the walls look almost alive, changing and moving as my perspective shifts and comes into reality.

I am starting to get my bearings. The door is halfway open, giving the most light and showing the path to my exit, which is the only direction I'm interested in at this exact moment.

As I shift my gaze toward him, the memories of last night come crashing back. His exposed shoulder muscles are round and smooth. He is just as beautiful in his sleep as he is awake. Maybe more so.

The presence of the man sleeping beside me, the man I didn't even know when I woke up yesterday morning, serves as a stark reminder of the choice we both made in the heat of the moment. Or rather, the choice we didn't make. We acted mindlessly, letting things unfold. With a single, unexpected kiss that rendered me incapable of thinking, our bodies took over.

Mixed emotions flood my mind as I try to process exactly what happened. There's a sense of excitement there, for sure. I had just made love for the first time in over a year. Simultaneously, there's a tinge of regret and pride rushing through me.

Then the realization that I have no idea who this man is or what I should do now cripples me.

The insecurity of how to proceed from here gives me a panicky feeling. In the bed, in the heat of passion, my inse-curities were nowhere to be found. But now, with the light of day, both of us with a bit of sleep in us, that doesn't feel realistic.

It's like I'm going through all of the emotions of grief right here before I even take the first step of the day. We are staying here together for several nights going forward, so I need to get my head straight. What an awkward conun-drum I have invited in by not thinking through what this would mean after the heat of the moment.

I move over to slide out of the side of the bed, trying not to disturb him with my micro-movements. I clench my teeth as if that somehow makes my movements less perceptible. Mr. Bojangles must still be in the living room, and I am sure he is wondering where I am.

I remember that Grayson said he has a meeting this morning, and I wonder if I should wake him or let him fend for himself. I search frantically with my eyes in the almost dark, gray room for some of my clothes or at least something to cover myself with. I cannot make out enough to see anything that will help.

I see what looks like it could be my Lululemon leggings on the floor. Everything looks like a shade of charcoal in here, so it is hard to know for sure.

Taking a deep breath, I rise from the bed and tiptoe towards the door, completely exposed, hoping he doesn't stir. I decide to leave the leggings for now and just make a run for my bedroom, where I know where clothes are.

The physical exhaustion and emotional weight of our explosive connection and busy, late night hits me as soon as I become vertical. I pause to let the dizziness subside.

As my mind flashes back to some of the more sensual moments, I remind myself of the importance of not over-thinking any of it. It was a moment of passion. It doesn't have to mean anything beyond that.

Once I reach the better-lit living area, my eyes are a few seconds behind in recalibration. Strangely, the extra light causes my eyes to go black for a split moment.

Mr. Bojangles is sleeping on the makeshift pallet I made for him on the floor in front of the now-extinguished fireplace. He looks like a picture from an ad, curled perfectly in the disheveled quilt, a sisal rug making up the frame.

My mind flashes back to the moment he pulled his shirt over his head, and I feel a wetness grow between my bare legs. His touch on my body was electric. Maybe it was the lack of time in between or the deliriousness of the late night and frigid temps. Whatever the case, that was quite possibly the best sex I have ever had in my life.

Mr. Bojangles looks up when I approach and probably wonders why I don't have any clothes on. He gets up and stretches. I would typically stop to pet him, but I make haste to get upstairs to get dressed before Grayson catches me wandering around his house in the nude.

I am determined to face him this morning with resilience and self-assurance as long as I'm clothed. Whatever that was and what comes today, we are two adults. Humans, at that. We all have needs, and we just both happened to meet in a perfect storm.

But something inside me feels like it was more than that....

The stairs squeak as I take the first step. I take them two at a time, wanting badly to get up there before he wakes. I flashback to yesterday when I was trying to get through the house without alerting him, but under very different circumstances.

The morning light is warm, still brightening and filling the bedroom. I collapse on the bed, naked as a jaybird. The cold comforter on my bare skin is like a plunge in the ocean in March. Refreshing, energizing. I hear Mr. Bojangles' collar jingle as he enters the room.

I'm typically an early-to-bed, early-to-rise type of person. Unless I am working on a new manuscript, of course. On some of those nights, I might find myself awake until the sun rises, the story flowing out of me so strongly I can't stop typing. If those moments come, I don't stifle them.

But last night, it was all about Grayson Sterling. I was held captive by his eyes. I was eager to peel back his layers, to touch his chiseled chest. But it came down to the eyes. That was the catalyst. Azure blue eyes, deep like the ocean. And just as intense.

The square jaw and strong hands didn't disappoint, either. A shudder runs through me as I remember his large hands running down my bare sides. An electric current rises from my toes to my clit. I can feel it pulsing. I reach my hand down to touch myself, turned on and eager for his touch again. I think of him as I explore the places no one else has touched in far too long, imagining him touching me again, not myself.

Immediately, my body shudders, and I pull a pillow onto my face. I ball up into the fetal position and hold my hand between my legs until my body calms. I needed that.

After a few minutes of taking it all in and enjoying the moment, I get up to use the restroom and find something to put on.

"I know you need to go to the bathroom, too, Buddy, don't you? We will go outside. Just give me a minute."

With the mention of the word "outside," Mr. B.'s backside starts dancing so fast that his front can't keep up.

By now, the sun is mainly over the horizon, and the light is coming in fully. I love starting my day with the morning light. I wake up early regardless of what's happening, even if I want to sleep in. It makes for a fresh and inviting start to my day. Something about my waning sleep mingled with the sunshine, both growing at inverse proportions, is magical.

I can tell by how cool it is in the house that it must be a pretty chilly morning. If I were only basing it on the sunshine and lack of clouds over the ocean, I would say it is warm. But I have woken up enough mornings here over the years to know that a bright, sunny morning in the spring does not equal a warm day.

I pull a chunky open-front sweater over my t-shirt and sweatpants and hunt for my slippers. Then I catch a glimpse of myself in the tall mirror leaning against the wall to the side of the bed and think twice.

Whatever happened between Grayson and me has nothing to do with my beauty. But I still have the urge to up my morning game. Just in case I see him. I don't want him to think I am some semi-homeless person. Even though I totally am right now.

I dig through my bag and pull out my fitted Levi's and a drapey, long-sleeved cardigan. I pull off the first sweater and replace it with the cuter one. So, I am still me with just a little sprucing up of my original outfit. I grab a scarf for extra warmth and head down the stairs with Mr. Bojangles for our morning potty sesh.

My stomach grumbles. I realize I never had a proper dinner last night and that it is empty. I remember all of the breakfast food I bought when we arrived. Going to the grocery store when I am hungry always ends up with me overdoing it.

This time, that overindulgence will allow me to make breakfast for Grayson this morning.

Or would that come across as desperate?

Who wouldn't want breakfast made for him, right? If I am staying in his home, in his bedroom, the least I could do is make him a breakfast to start his day. He won't have to eat or interact with me if he doesn't want to.

At the bottom of the stairs, the room is dead silent. I don't hear Grayson stirring at all, so I slide in my socks to the front door, trying not to make a sound, and quietly unlock it. I grab Mr. B's leash and poop bags. He pushes past me as soon as the door opens, almost knocking me off my feet, and jets down the stairs. I guess he really had to go.

The air is brisk, as I suspected it would be. A fine mist of moisture rests on all of the surfaces as the sunshine attempts to evaporate the morning dew. I wrap my cardigan tighter around me and follow my leader down the wooden stairs.

He is already on the grass below doing his business. He squats while looking up at me as if I am interrupting his privacy. My socks are now damp from the morning grass. Why didn't I put on shoes? "Don't mind me, Buddy. I am just here to pick it up."

With that, he bounds up and starts sniffing around the lawn. I bend down to pick up his morning deposit.

The gulls are out early. The air is crisp and lovely. I finally and confidently decide that I will make Grayson breakfast after all. I need to eat, and that is the main objective. I'll make enough for him, too, and he can decide for himself if he wants it. I'm not responsible for what he thinks it means.

There are a dozen eggs, a loaf of bread, and some avocados and local tomatoes. There is no way I could eat everything before the week was up anyway. Now it looks like I'll be able to use it all up for sure.

"You ready to go inside, Bud? It's chilly out here for me." Mr. B. looks up at me as if to say, "What?!" And then resumes sniffing. He is telling me he isn't ready to go back inside yet. But I am the boss, and I am hungry and cold.

"You want to eat?" With the word "eat," his ears perk up, and he looks at me with a smile in his caramel-brown eyes. I knew that would do it.

He darts for the front steps, sliding slightly at the bottom from the momentum. It's incredible to me how smart he is. Once again, I follow him back inside. I drop the little baggy on the bottom front step with the intention to come back to it and throw it in the outside trash can.

———

7:02 *am EST*

IT'S JUST after seven now, and pull out the shredded cheddar cheese, the salt cellar, and the pepper grinder. I am finishing up scrambling the eggs, and the grits will be done in about two minutes. Everything came together as if I planned this breakfast.

I grab the fresh-squeezed orange juice and pour it into a glass jug. It looks better than putting out the store-bought box, almost like I got up and squeezed the oranges myself.

"Crap!" I say when I smell bread burning under the broiler. "Dammit." I pull out the cookie sheet, and sure enough, the toast is black and crispy. I dump the mess in the trashcan and slam the pan on the stovetop a little too aggressively.

Oops. I forgot that I am trying to be quiet. Grayson said he was leaving around eight, so I imagine he is up anyway. But dammit. Things have been going so well, but he will only notice the smell of burnt toast.

I realize I am letting myself care way more than I need to about what he needs, wants, and thinks. What about the notion that I am not responsible for what he thinks? What about what I need and want and think? I'm pathetic.

"Everything okay in here," Grayson asks as he walks into the kitchen. For the love of all things holy, this man is sexier than I remember.

He saunters down the hall in his bare feet, fitted khaki pants, and crisp, white button-down shirt. His hair is damp and brushed back, a few cheeky strands falling down, framing his handsome face. I pinch myself to see if I am still snuggled up in bed dreaming.

"I am so sorry about that. I realized I had all of this food so I thought I would make breakfast in case you wanted to grab something before you head out. I am really sorry if I disturbed you."

"No worries at all. I think you may have something burning in the oven, though."

He gives me a half smile, just enough to show off his dimples. I am a puddle with this man. And my face flushes, embarrassed that I am making a great impression with my burnt toast. Super inviting.

"Oh, yeah, I forgot about the toast. But don't worry, I already got it out, so your house is safe. I do admit I am not the best cook, but I can assure you I won't burn your house down while you're gone."

He offers up a noise. I'm not sure what to call it. Is that a friendly laugh or an annoyed grunt? I think I detect a smile on his face.

"I trust you. Is there anything I can do to help?"

"No, thank you. As a matter of fact, everything is done, and I made more than enough for myself. Please don't feel like you have to eat, but if you're hungry, I made stone-ground grits and scrambled eggs and cut up avocado and local heirloom tomatoes. The second batch of toast will be ready any second. Shit!"

I rush to the oven and open it. Sure enough, I've burnt the second round of toast! How did I do this?! Again? At least it's not black like the first batch.

"Well, there will be toast in a minute." I open the half-gone loaf of bread and pull out four more slices for the third time this morning. I put them on the cookie sheet, put a little butter on them, and put them back in.

When I turn back around he is gone. I guess the burnt bread was a non-starter. Geez, I feel like an idiot. Everything is out, and I told him there is more than enough for him. I think that is all I can do. Now, should I awkwardly wait for him to join me, or grab a plate and eat and hope he comes back soon?

FIFTEEN

Grayson
_____

7:29 am EST

THIS IS NOT how I like to start my days. If the smell of my house burning down isn't enough, she thinks that after a roll in the hay last night, we will dine together this morning? Nice thought.

You aren't the first woman to think I want to settle down with her. But it's not going to happen.

I probably wouldn't be so irritated if I hadn't just gotten an email from Bartles outlining how Claire pulled off this scheme. It is clouding my thoughts, overshadowing my meeting this morning.

I don't have the emotional capital to try to navigate whatever this is. Or isn't. While I genuinely find her intriguing and strikingly beautiful, I don't have the energy to delve further. We essentially live in two different worlds.

Now that I know my kitchen isn't on fire and she seems somewhat competent, I will make myself invisible until Olivier arrives. Looking at our itinerary for today, it's clear that we will not be done until after dinner, and I probably won't get back here until close to midnight again. I'll make sure not to have my nightcap on the deck tonight.

Once it is a minor indiscretion, it is easily written off. Twice becomes a habit. That is when they start getting clingy.

As far as I am concerned, that will not happen again. With that thought, my mind jumps back to my hands tracing her body, and I get a chill. I feel myself growing in my pants. While it was amazing, and I do find her quite intriguing, I need to keep our interaction professional and at arm's length.

My phone buzzes in my pocket, and I reach down to fish it out. A text message from Thomas Earhardt at Coastal Horizon Development Corp pops up.

> Good morning, Grayson. I'm very sorry for the late cancellation, but I just got a call from the city planner. He had an emergency out of town. I left a message with your assistant last night, but I wanted to text you directly since I didn't hear back. He will be back tonight, so if tomorrow morning works, we can make that happen.

Motherfucker. Doesn't he know that I am not here on vacation? I made last-minute changes to meet with him. Then he cancels like it is nothing. I feel my face red as I work out how to respond.

Maybe he's just fucking with me to see how much I'll grovel. He will quickly learn that I've given him more than I give most.

Dammit. Everly is still on vacation, so that means Claire would have gotten that message. I have not yet decided how to deal with Claire, so I haven't been in touch, but there is no doubt she knows that I know what she's been up to.

I need to get back to L.A. I am suddenly feeling very anxious and scattered. Everly will be back on Monday, but I will not be waiting until then. Thomas Earhardt and the pencil dick city planner will have to wait until my schedule opens up. I know the city needs this project to happen, so he can do some of the groveling now.

I don't have the time or the inclination to waste an entire day here waiting on him. I text Olivier.

> Morning meeting xled—no need to drive to Virginia this morning. Stand by.

It is truly pathetic how much I have come to depend on Everly. My ineffectiveness with her on vacation is shameful. The weak link is Claire. That situation has to be handled ASAP. Best that I fly back home today.

My indiscretion with Hollis last night is not helping this situation. Staying here could test my self-restraint. The last thing I need is to invite another complicated situation into my life. I need to focus on work and my real life, which is three thousand miles away.

Now, as for Claire.

I pull up her number and press send. It goes straight to voicemail. I try it again a few times, just in case it's a connection thing. Then I leave her a message.

"Good morning, Claire. This is Grayson Sterling. Please give me a call as soon as you get this message. Thanks."

As I end the call, I know she isn't going to call me back. She always answers my calls. That she didn't even have it on lets me know everything I need to know. But I already know all of this. She has checked out. I send Andrew Bartles a quick text.

> I have an urgent need. The fraud situation with the Outer Banks house needs handling. I suspect Claire has flown the coop. I want to go after her with the full force of the law and fire her properly. Coordinate with HR and legal to make sure we do this correctly. I'll be here until Tuesday. Please provide me with a plan of action and get back to me.

I pull out my laptop and start going through my emails. There is one from HR titled Claire Stackhouse:

Blaire Polisickk – Human Resources

Sterling Development Group, Inc. (SDG)

To: Grayson Sterling

CC: Everly, Claire Stackhouse, Blanton, Eric REMS

Subject: Investigation AJ2987

Dear Mr. Sterling,

An internal investigation has been initiated after a complaint by employee Claire Stackhouse. It was carried

92

out as per company policy. Ms. Sackhouse alleges CEO Grayson Sterling made sexual advances toward her on three separate occasions:

10/11/18

1/5/19

2/1/19

She has provided documentation and has a list of witnesses and other corroborating evidence. All discovery documentation will be available through contacting Human Resources or your attorney.

We have hired the law firm REMS out of Atlanta, GA, to help do the forensic research and to represent the SDG in any action as we advance. All correspondence regarding this should reference Investigation AJ2987 and copy all parties on this email.

We have advised Ms. Stackhouse to retain her own counsel, but her employment contract does afford her an attorney paid for by the SDG in the event there is a work-related incident. The contract also states that she will be responsible for all attorney fees if she is found to have made unfounded claims.

She has been assigned an HR agent who will work directly with her through this investigation process and is a fiduciary to her only. That person will still report to SDG HR but will only represent her until our investigation is done.

All related questions for Investigation AJ2987 should be directed to your HR representative, Blaire Polisickk at SDG, and Eric Blanton at REMS.

Sincerely,

Blaire Polisickk

d/cc: list of witnesses, receipts, travel documents, employment contract

Fuck me sideways. I throw my Smart water bottle against the wall. The loosely screwed-on top pops off, and water goes everywhere. A stream drips slowly down the wood-sided wall while I absorb this. My own fucking company, and I get a letter from HR like this.

My mind flashes back to the HR consultant we hired last year that set up this independent system. I own this fucking company, and I get a letter like this with no heads-up? I could choke someone right now I am so mad - at everyone.

I try to think of how I should respond. My blood is boiling, and I feel like my head is going to explode. Right now, I need to focus on Claire, and then I can decide who to fire in HR.

I hear Hollis in the living room talking to Mr. Bojangles. I have an unnatural desire to go to her to seek her comfort. I hardly know her, but for some reason, I am drawn to her for a clear head.

Then, the realization hit me like a hurricane. What might Hollis think if she were to hear about this? It is one hundred percent untrue, but that doesn't stop some opportunist from making false accusations. Not only is there an opportunity for a payday to keep it out of the news, but Claire needs a diversion for her criminal acts.

Well played, I suppose. It will at least buy her some time. And possibly a way out of this. What she didn't count on is that I always take meticulous notes and never allow myself to be alone with a female employee in a precarious situation for this precise reason. I have heard too many stories of someone trying to frame someone with financial means to think that I am immune.

After my heart rate comes down a little, I pull out my phone and go to each of the dates noted in the email to see exactly where I was and what kind of interaction I might have had with her.

She is going to rue the day she decided to fuck with me. I will fry her.

I finally can't take it anymore without Everly. I need to explain, and she needs to get on this. I text her:

> I did everything I could to handle this without bothering you, but we have a situation. If you haven't checked your email today, you will know why I needed to reach out when you do. I need thirty minutes of your time to go over this. Check your email and let me know a time today we can speak. -G.

Once I send that, I see I have an unread text.

One from Andrew Bartles:

> I'm on it, boss. I will do some research and be in touch today.

I pack my things and text Olivier:

I need a private flight out to LA today. If my jet is still parked in Virginia, find me a pilot. Money is no object. Just make it happen today. Pick me up here once that is scheduled. Let me know. Thanks. –G

SIXTEEN

Hollis

10:13 am EST

IT IS obvious Grayson isn't a morning person. I was presumptuous to think that little tryst last night would mean anything today. I am obviously a little rusty when it comes to deciphering men and their unspoken rules.

He left while I was upstairs. I heard the front door close, and when I came down, his stuff was gone, and he was nowhere in sight. That was jarring.

As I clean up the remnants of the ill-fated breakfast, the urgent need to get out of here comes over me like a tidal wave. I feel like an idiot and am full, needing to walk off the meal for two I just consumed.

Grayson hasn't gotten back to me with that address. Maybe he was just posturing about having a rental. Was that a ploy to get in my pants? I hope not because that would be two letdowns.

I walk upstairs and wash up after my solitary breakfast. I decide to put on another layer and a fleece for our next walk. There's no need to worry about looking cute.

"I know, Buddy. Men are always sending mixed signals. I'm not ready for being out in the wild with them. I think it will just be you and me, and I am fine with that!"

Mr. Bojangles wags his tail. His kind eyes are my comfort. I pat him on the head, and the warm touch of his soft red hair comforts me. I bend down and kiss him on the side of his head. Damn, I love this dog.

We walk downstairs together, his devotion for me palpable. I need that extra boost at this moment. Letting myself sleep with this man, this stranger, was naive at best. Expecting we could somehow enjoy each other's company this morning was stupid. I feel tears welling but manage to push them back. There's no way I'm getting emotional over this.

We head to the back sliding door, and as I go to open it, my phone buzzes. I reach into the front pocket pouch on my fleece to fish it out. There is a text from Grayson:

> The address is 7 Allgood Road, Duck. As I mentioned, please do not knock on the door. If Mrs. Zeddleman is outside, you're welcome to mention you're looking at the house, but otherwise, please ride by only. We can discuss if you're interested in exploring further.

No mention of last night. No apologies for missing breakfast, or for walking off without any word today, for that matter.

There was no warmth or any signs that we even interacted. At least I got that address, and it wasn't a big fat lie. If this works out, I will consider it a win.

I still feel a tiny ache in my heart at the reminder of the blow-off. I need to remember to guard myself better in the future.

Mr. B and I will head that way instead of walking on the beach. I pull up the map on my phone and see it is only seven-tenths of a mile away walking. That is less than we would do on the beach, so it's perfect.

Having this to explore and the possibility of finding my new home is exhilarating. I'm not sure about the landlord, but I wouldn't be dealing with him anyway, based on what I gathered last night.

The blue sky and bright sunshine are beautiful and bright, with hardly a cloud in sight as we head out, walking briskly to work up a little heat. I am excited to see the rental and what's around it.

We arrive in less than ten minutes. The house is simply adorable. There is a little white picket fence around the front yard. A tiny traditional blue clapboard-sided cottage with red shutters and white trim. It couldn't be more quaint and quintessential beachy. It is just perfect.

I immediately spot the brick chimney coming out of the roof, smoke billowing out. I could cry. I am so excited for the good fortune of all of this. That he only wants $1,200 a month for this blows me away.

I can barely contain my excitement.

There is no sign of Mrs. Zeddleman, although I do see the warm glow of lights inside. As requested, I won't disturb her, but it doesn't matter what is inside. I want to text Grayson right now to let him know I will take it, but I restrain myself. He isn't giving off the same warm and welcoming vibes he was last night.

Instead, I do a little more exploring. I am now confidently familiar with what is within walking distance with all the walking I have been doing the last few days. There is a grocery store to the right, heading north, and a tiny post office around the corner. The beach is three blocks to the east. I couldn't have dreamed of a better place for my fresh start.

Mr. Bojangles and I head left since I am unsure what exactly is in this direction. I'm walking slower now, taking in all of the small ranches and old beach-town-looking homes on both sides. The oak trees with Spanish Moss down the neighborhood streets are stunning. I've always loved this place, but I feel like I am seeing it with even more wonder and awe now.

I spot a little cafe ahead with a dog bowl outside, signifying that furry friends are welcome. This is my place. We walk up, and Mr. Bojangles goes straight for a few laps of water. I peer inside and see a few people. Once he is done, we walk in.

There is a bell on the door. It jingles as the door opens. A young lady is at the counter and offers a big smile as we walk in.

"Good morning to you on this chilly morning! And who is this handsome man?" She asks as she walks around to greet Mr. Bojangles. "Can I get y'all anything? We have happy doggy popsicles, but it might be a little too cold for that."

"This is Mr. Bojangles, and he would love a doggy popsicle. He doesn't get cold. And I would love your biggest, hottest latte, please, because I do."

"Coming right up. Have a seat wherever you like, and I will bring them to you."

We find a seat in the front corner, perfect for people-watching and to get him out of the way.

Eighty-five pounds of girth takes up more floor space than you might imagine.

I realize the name of the cafe is Sacred Grounds. That is precisely how I feel about this place. This whole place. The beach. The town. And now my new beginning.

There's a perfect spot in the window to sit and write all day with my sidekick in tow. I am overcome with a sense that everything is lining up and will be the exact spot I need to grow, heal, and rediscover myself.

I pull out my phone to text Grayson, his comfort level be damned:

> I love the house! I definitely want it, and I am fine waiting until the timing works for you and Mrs. Zeddleman. Please let me know who I need to contact to sign and pay whatever you need to secure it. Thank you!

I sit back and sigh. I feel so grateful for the universe delivering all of this to me. It is all I can do to fight breaking down into the cry I have in me. It's been trying to bubble to the surface since yesterday. Luckily, the adorable woman walks up with my latte and Mr. B's treat, and the tears retreat again.

"Here you go, sweetheart," she says as she puts the large pottery mug on the table. "And this is for you, Mister." She bends down to get at his eye level. Mr. Bojangles is alert and smiling, excited for the deliciousness she is holding for him but not snatching as he has been taught. He is such a good boy.

She sets it and the small plastic plate on the sandy wood floor in front of him. As soon as she pulls her hand away, he goes to town. I think it was three licks and a gobble. He wasn't letting that get away from him.

"Hi, I am Kendall. Are you visiting?"

She sits down in the chair across from me. Her warmth and kindness radiate from her smile. I have a strange desire to hug her.

"Well, actually, I was. Or I should say, I am visiting. But I think I am moving here in the next few weeks, just down the road. I'm Hollis. And you already met Mr. Bojangles. It's so nice to meet you."

I reach out my hand to shake hers. Kendall is someone I would like to be friends with. I need a friend right now.

"How exciting! Welcome! I hope we will get to see lots of you two."

"If everything works out with the rental, you definitely will. I am a writer, and this is a perfect place for me to sit and be inspired and write and ingest lots of caffeine."

"How cool! I love it. We would love to have you both, and we will make sure to keep you full of all of the caffeine you can drink and doggie treats Mr. Bojangles wants!"

"Do you know Mrs. Zeddleman down the street? I hope to be renting her house."

"Of course I do! She is right over there," she points to a table on the far side. The cutest little lady is sitting at a small two-top table with the entire newspaper open and taking up more room than her and the table she is sitting at.

I am suddenly embarrassed since it is not official. I should have known that everyone knows each other in such a small place. I feel my cheeks fill with color.

"Mrs. Zeddleman actually works here a few hours each week, and we are so sad to lose her. But we are all so happy for her that she is moving closer to her family in Charlotte. She promises to come visit us."

"I may have spoken out of place. I have not officially signed any lease. I just met the owner yesterday and found out it was coming available."

My mind flashes to Grayson's bare chest and the v-shape his abs and lats make as they travel down. My body tingles at the thought.

"I think I got a little excited about it all. Now I feel like I may have overstepped my bounds."

"Oh, for heaven's sake. Don't worry a bit! Mrs. Zeddleman is truly the nicest person. May I introduce you?"

"Sure, I guess. If you don't think it will be an imposition. I know how touchy moving can be, especially if she is attached. I don't want to intrude on anyone."

"Stop it! She would love to meet you. Please let me make an introduction. She will adore Mr. Bojangles, too!"

I follow her lead as we walk to the table with the petite older lady.

"Mrs. Zeddleman. You won't believe who is here and is my new best friend! Hollis and Mr. Bojangles are hoping to rent your house when you move. Hollis, Mrs. Zeddleman. Mrs. Zeddleman, Hollis. I'm sorry, Hollis, I didn't catch your last name."

"Hollis Mitchell. Hi, Mrs. Zeddleman. Please pardon my interruption of your paper reading. I was just telling Kendall I was hoping to rent your house, and she said you were here and insisted we meet. It is a pleasure to meet you. I walked by your house this morning, and it is positively darling. I love all of the gardening you have done. It is a little doll house!"

"Hollis! It is so nice to make your acquaintance. I am thrilled to meet the new occupant. It is a special place, and I know you will love it as much as I have."

"Well, nothing official yet. I just met Grayson Sterling, and he told me about it last night. It all just happened by chance. No planning on either of our parts. I haven't signed a lease yet."

"Oh, Grayson Sterling is a sheep in wolf's clothing, isn't he? He tries to be such a busy, important man, but deep down, he is a teddy bear. And not hard on the eyes, too," she says with a big smile and a wink. I can see she has affection for him.

I feel a stirring in my stomach as she says this. A tightness in my heart catches me off guard. It's more like a wolf in sheep's clothing.

She offers to take me to see the inside of the house. I couldn't say yes quickly enough.

She had her bike but walked it to walk with Mr. Bojangles and me. She pointed out several of the homes and explained their history.

The house is as cute on the inside as it is on the outside. Maybe cuter if possible.

The red wood door with a glass window on the top half opens into a cozy little foyer. I noticed she didn't unlock it. The living area to the left opens onto a dining table and a small back door. An old cast iron wood stove with an exposed pipe runs up to the ceiling.

"Does that little stove keep your whole house warm?"

"Yes, it does, and it is marvelous! I can put wood in there in the morning, and it will last all day. And my gas bill is next to nothing because of it."

"How neat is that! I love it."

To the right of the dining area is a small galley kitchen complete with natural wood cabinets and an old-timey white enamel refrigerator, gas stove, and butcher-block countertops. She keeps it as neat as a pin, with everything in its place. I am in love with this house. And Mrs. Zeddleman.

SEVENTEEN

Grayson
_____

11:01 am EST

MY JET IS STILL at the airport, and Olivier found a pilot for me. My regular pilot couldn't fly me home, but it appears there is an Uber-type program for pilots, and he was able to secure one reasonably quickly. We are leaving in an hour. I'll be back in L.A. by noon.

This whole debacle has made two things clear to me. First, I need two backup assistants. Second, and more disturbing, I have become way too dependent on my assistants and need to learn how to do things for myself again.

Through all of the havoc and mess swirling around me right now, my mind continues to return to Hollis. It must be a lack of sleep, but I still have to make a conscious effort to put her and last night out of my mind. I do need to text her back, though.

I will have Everly, my assistant, contact you on Monday. She will get the information from you for a background check. I'm sure all is fine there, but that is policy. And then she will draw up the lease agreement for you to sign, assuming all is well there. I am heading back to California, so you have the house to yourself. Thanks for an enjoyable night last night.

God, I am an imbecile. Thanks for an enjoyable night? Why did I say that? Haven't they come up with a way to unsend a text?

———

THURSDAY, *April 4*

11:53 am PST

I'M SITTING in my attorney's office, my mind a whirlwind of emotions and confusion. It's been weeks since I stumbled upon Claire's scheme to rent out my vacation home without my consent, and the situation has escalated far beyond what I could have imagined.

I've provided Bentley Cross, my attorney, with all the evidence I could gather. It clearly shows that what Claire is alleging regarding the inappropriate contact is entirely unfounded and untrue. I'm confident that I can prove my innocence.

Bentley, a sharp and experienced litigator, studies the documents on her desk. "Grayson, I've carefully reviewed your case and believe we have a strong defense. There's substantial evidence that you had nothing to do with what Claire alleges. However, there's a settlement offer on the table that might be worth considering."

I'm not settling with that bitch.

She proceeds to lay out Claire's proposal, her voice measured and cautious. "Claire's attorney is suggesting that if you drop any charges against her and refrain from pursuing legal action against her, she'll withdraw the sexual harassment claim. This would effectively put an end to the matter. It would save you time, money, and a lot of stress."

Bentley's words hang in the air, and I can feel the weight of the decision. On one hand, I know I'm in the right, and I want to clear my name in court.

But on the other, I also understand the damage to my reputation that this ordeal is causing, not to mention the exorbitant legal fees I'll incur during a prolonged legal battle. Claire is cunning. I am sure she orchestrated all of this, likely anticipating that I'd be backed into a corner as her escape plan.

I lean back in my chair and run my fingers through my hair, feeling the tension in my shoulders. Oddly, for some reason, my mind goes to Hollis. We haven't spoken since our night last month. I have restrained myself several times from calling her. It wouldn't be fair to her.

"What are the possible outcomes if I choose to fight her in court?"

Bentley takes a deep breath, choosing her words carefully. "If we go to court, we can likely prove your innocence, but it could drag on for months, even years. The cost in attorney fees, not to mention the toll on your reputation, could be substantial. And there's always the risk of unfore-seen developments. It's a gamble."

The money is not my concern. But I don't want this hanging over me for years. And the longer this goes on, the more damage it does to me. Not to mention, I don't put it past her that she will try to wage a public smear campaign on me if I push her hand.

I ponder the options, the conflict between seeking justice and protecting myself gnawing at my conscience. Claire orchestrated this entire situation, and now she's offering a way out, but I know it's all part of her plan.

My phone buzzes, and I pull it out as I absorb what Bentley is saying. As if on cue, it is a text Hollis. I feel all of the blood leave my entire head and pool at my feet. Seeing her name on my phone is a surreal feeling. We haven't spoken since March, but I still think of her regularly.

> Hey, there. Just wanted to let you know I'm loving your house on the island. I appreciate you telling me about it. If you're ever here, I would love to meet for coffee or something.

What in the absolute hell is this? My mouth is dry as I try to make sense of this. Out of the blue. But still a deep thread after all of this time.

Immediately, I shudder at the thought of what she would think of me if she somehow saw something about it in the news. That wouldn't be a stretch with my presence in Virginia Beach and the extensive development going on there. I normally don't care what people think, but this thought grabs me.

I think about our conversations that night, and I would actually like to know what her advice would be in this situation. The timing of her text feels like a sign. I can't believe she is reaching out to me after how much of a jerk I was to leave without speaking that morning.

What a first phone call that would be. I can imagine it now, "Hey Hollis, it's me, Grayson. You know, the guy who slept with you and then left without a word? Well, anyway, I need some advice. Remember the lady who stole my house and falsely rented it to you? Well, she is trying to use a sexual harassment claim to get out of it. Should I let her manipulate me and get out of it or take her to the cleaners?"

Yeah, that's not gonna work. Why was I such an asshole? I power off my screen and put my phone back in my pocket.

———

MONDAY, *November 18*

8:02 am PST/ 11:02 am EST

EVERLY KNOCKS ON MY DOOR. "Grayson, we have a situation at the cottage at the Outer Banks."

I roll my eyes. I don't have the time or the mental capacity to hear about petty issues at a small cottage two thousand miles away from me.

And then it hits me. Hollis. Mr. Bojangles. My heart sinks.

"What's going on? Is everyone okay?"

I feel sick at the worst-case scenarios rushing through my mind.

"Everyone is fine. Normally, I wouldn't bother you with this, but there is a major issue, and I want to make you aware. It appears there was a fire in the attic. The new tenant, Hollis Mitchell, called to let me know she was home and realized what was happening before it got out of control, thank goodness."

Hollis Mitchell. Time stands still. I think I forget to breathe for a few seconds. I look at my watch, doing the math for the time there. Most importantly, she is okay.

"The fire department is there now, and it is under control as far as we can tell. Everything is covered in water, though. I am sending out an adjuster to survey the damage to see what needs to be done to ensure everything is structurally sound."

"For fucks sake." Hearing this takes the wind out of my chest. "That sounds really bad. Do you know anything about the damage? What caused it? Thank you for letting me know. Please keep me informed about everything regarding that. I want to know everything."

The moment I hear her name, a rush of emotions surges within me. The thought of the sound of Hollis's voice immediately hits me. I can't help but picture her sitting on the deck that night, her one hand on Mr. Bojangles, the other on her mug of tea, as she laughed at my stupid story about building the beach house. Her auburn hair framing her face. Her eyes gazing up at the dark night sky.

"I know that the roof is mostly gone, and I'm not sure how far into the main home the fire went. It is happening in real-time, and the fire department is still there, making sure everything is contained, but I will know more soon."

I shake my head, trying to refocus on the conversation with Everly. "When is the adjuster scheduled to go out? I wonder if I should fly out there to make certain it is handled properly."

"Oh, I don't think you need to go out there. I am taking care of it and will report what we find out. I don't see how you going there would do anything more."

I'm sure I just blew her mind by suggesting I fly out to oversee something like this. She is over all issues with the residential rentals, and I can't remember the last time she even told me about anything with one of them. I'm only guessing she told me about this one because the fire damage could be more significant than a plumbing issue or something easy to fix. And there is a safety issue.

"And to answer your question, the adjuster is going out this afternoon. Regardless, I've told him to let me know as soon as possible, especially if extensive damage renders it unsafe to live in."

Everly proceeds to outline the details of the situation further, what she knows. A slow burn. My mind continues to drift.

I am coming in and out of what she is saying, trying to determine if I should handle this myself rather than letting someone else. She says there is nothing more I can do, but I am fully aware that if I am present, people tend to be more on point.

I am lost in thoughts of that night back in March, replaying our conversation and the chemistry between us. I remember fondly how she spoke about her love for the island, the sea, and the stars in the night sky.

Rather than fading from my mind, my thoughts have become more obsessive about her. If I could go back in time, I would do that morning differently.

I thought it was just a physical thing. I think deep down, I've always known it was something more. Maybe that is what scares me so much. I never continue to think about a woman the way I have with her.

As Everly wraps up her explanation, I nod, regaining my composure. "Alright, let's get a repair team out there as soon as possible once you have a handle on the damage and what needs to be done. We need to make sure Hollis is comfortable and her home is safe. In the meantime, let's go ahead and get her a suite at The Sanderling."

Hollis's name continues to echo in my mind long after Everly leaves my office. I can't help but wonder if fate is teasing me, reminding me of the woman I met on that night and let slip through my fingers. Yet, the reality remains. She lives on the other side of the country, and work and responsibilities consume my life. What kind of life could we have together? I can't afford to let my thoughts wander down that path, as tempting as it may be.

EIGHTEEN

Hollis

12:03 pm EST

I AM STANDING OUTSIDE at noon in late November in my Ugg slippers and sweatpants. November in Duck is no joke. The baby kicks. I place my hand on my huge belly.

I want to reach out to Grayson, but he has made it glaringly clear he doesn't want to have contact with me. I reached out in April to figure out a way to tell him that I was pregnant. And he didn't respond. Nothing.

"Yessir," I tell the fire chief. "I was sitting in the living room reading. My dog started pacing, so I thought he had to go outside. He never does that, so I worried he was having a bathroom emergency.

I jumped up to avoid an accident and opened the door. As soon as I did, I could smell a strong smell of smoke. I walked out to see if I could see something burning nearby.

That's when I saw flames on the roof. I called 911 immediately and did not go back into the house."

The cool, moist beach air is cutting through my clothes, even with all of the adrenaline and the heat coming off of the house.

"That was quick thinking. If you hadn't been home, there is a good chance you would have lost your home and everything in it. You had minutes, tops, before the flames came inside. You must have a guardian angel."

I do. Mr. Bojangles. He is the hero here, once again.

Everything in it. That phrase is playing on a loop in my mind. The fire chief is explaining something I am sure is important, but that is all I can think about. I chose not to go to Sacred Grounds this morning, like I do almost every morning, because my lower back is really hurting me. I was almost not here.

My chest tightens at the thought of not being home and Mr. Bojangles being here alone. I take him most of the time, but lately, everything hurts, so I have been leaving him at home. I don't care about the things. My house is still pretty bare. Things can be replaced. But if I had lost him, I don't think I would have survived.

"It looks like the wood stove exhaust pipe had come loose in the attic, and an ember escaped, landing on some old newspapers in the attic. Once something like that gets in an ideal environment like that – enclosed, dry, isolated – it's only a matter of time."

The wood stove. The panic inside of me grows. I always let the fire smolder in the night. I am rattled and feel like I need to sit down. I spot a lone chair that is out of place and doesn't belong in my yard.

"We have an ambulance here, and I would like for you to go to the hospital to be checked out. I know the smoke wasn't really in the house yet, but the fact that you are very pregnant calls for you to just play it safe. Is there someone that can take your dog for you while you take a ride up there?"

I sit down on the chair. I am guessing that someone must have brought it over to us. My head is spinning, and I feel a little loopy all of a sudden. All of this is a lot, and dealing with it by myself is almost too much. This is when I need a husband, even if we were just roommates—someone to hold my hand and let me know that everything will be okay.

"Yes, I will text her now. Thank you for everything. I will get in the ambulance once I rest a moment and get in touch with my friend about my dog. Is that okay?"

"Of course. Take your time. I am going to step over here to get an update."

I take my phone out of my back pocket and pull up Kendall's name. I realize my hands are shaking. I shoot her a quick text.

> Hey, girl. There was a fire at my house this morning. Everyone is okay, but the fire chief wants me to go to the hospital to be checked out. I know I am fine, but I don't have the wherewithal to argue. Can Mr. B. come up there to hang out with you until I get done? I need to know he is safe.

I put my phone down in my lap and hold my head. This is the first time since this all started unfolding over two hours ago that I have had a moment to myself. I can't stop the tears from flowing. I don't want anyone to see me crying, but I can't help myself.

Kendall texts me back right away.

> Baby girl! Are you okay?! I am so sorry!! Of course, I will care for Mr. Bojangles as if he were mine. Unlimited doggie popsicles. I want to hear everything, but I know you must have a lot going on. We can talk later. I asked Charity, and she said I can walk down to your house. I am almost there. See you soon.

I grab Mr. Bojangles' head and hug it tight to my chest. "Thank you, Buddy. You saved all of us."

As soon as the words get out of my mouth and the floodgates open. Ugly crying right here on this brown folding chair on my front lawn, facing what is left of my adorable little cottage. My fresh start, up in flames.

Just in time to hug me, Kendall walks up. I get up and walk towards her, Mr. Bojangles right beside me. She hugs me. The human touch I so desperately need. The tears come again, more ferocious this time. I thought I had gotten them all out.

"Baby girl, I am just so sorry. I am glad you are all safe. I don't even want to think about the worst-case scenario. Do you know what happened?"

"All I know is I was sitting in the chair in the front room reading when Mr. Bojangles started going crazy. I thought he was about to have an accident, so I ran outside to let him go. When we got out, I realized the roof was on fire. I had no idea inside. Not a clue. No smoke smell, nothing."

"Mr. Bojangles! You saved the day again! You deserve a medal! And you will definitely get unlimited doggie popsicles with Auntie Kendall today!"

Kendall reaches over and hugs me tightly, reassuring me again. She has been my lifesaver these last eight months. She is my ride-or-die, best friend, confidant, therapist. I am not sure I would be standing here if it weren't for her and Mr. B.

"I love you, girl. Thank you for always being there to pick up the pieces for me."

"You do not have to thank me! You know I would move mountains for you. You just keep yourself and that precious baby safe. You can always count on me."

After a few minutes of letting the tears flow, I compose myself. I've got this. I have to be strong and put my big girl pants back on. I have three to protect now. It's time to go to the hospital.

I watch as Kendall and Mr. Bojangles walk off towards the cafe. He turns his head to look back at me, still my protector.

I pull out my phone, and a text comes in at that exact moment. Grayson Sterling.

Hey. I just heard about the fire. I am so glad that you and Mr. Bojangles are okay. I want you to know that I am personally making sure everything is taken care of, and I've asked Everly to reserve a suite for you at The Sanderling. I'm so sorry.

I pick my jaw up off of the ground. It's been nine months since I have seen or heard from him. I am finding it hard to breathe at the moment.

Is he sorry that he left me knocked up with narry a peep? I am overcome with guilt that he has no idea that he has a baby boy coming any day. What kind of woman does that? My feeble attempt at a text wasn't enough. I am a terrible person.

NINETEEN

Grayson
———————

MY PHONE DOES a little dance on my desk's hard, smooth surface. The rapid click-click-click vibration startles me at first, loud and piercing in my otherwise quiet office. It's Everly. I pick it up immediately, unable to do anything else since hearing about the fire.

"Any news?" I answer the phone.

"I just hung up with the adjuster. He said the entire top portion of the house has to be pulled out and rebuilt. The inside has some smoke and water damage, but structurally, it is fine. He said the renovation would take about seven weeks and that everything could be set up to start within the next two weeks. That means ten to twelve weeks, allowing for unexpected delays, for the tenant to be out of there. Are you okay with me keeping her at The Sanderling until the end of January, or possibly into February, give or take?"

"Absolutely. Whatever it takes. I want to guarantee that everything is done right and that she is comfortable."

What she just described is worse than she made it seem this morning. This isn't good. And it could have been even worse. I am so glad everyone is safe. But there is something about it that makes me feel like I didn't do enough to protect her. I feel like I should be doing more to make it right now.

"Okay, will do. We are exploring contractors in North Carolina now."

"If we need to send in our crew, let's do that. I feel like three months is a long time. I have a crew that can knock that out in a month."

I open the file sitting on top of the pile on my desk to get the number of the contractor we used to build the beach house. He will be doing some of the framing on the Virginia Beach project. I want to see if he can fit us in and make it happen quicker.

"Also, please make sure Hollis Mitchell is okay with us putting her up for that long. Or, we can let her out of her lease if she prefers. Make sure she knows we will do whatever she needs to make this right. And please send her my sincere apologies."

I hang up and put my phone back on my desk. I can't focus on anything else.

She hasn't answered my text. I don't blame her. Another dagger to my gut that I shouldn't have waited for a tragedy to reach out to her.

I lean back in my desk chair and go through the whole series of events again. From March, when I met Hollis, to this morning, when I heard there was a fire at her house, It has been one helluva year. And this must be the coup de gras. Or at least, I hope it is.

I have a heavy feeling of foreboding weighing on me. I desperately want to reach out to Hollis again, but I know that is inappropriate. I left her hanging without another word almost a year ago. I was an ass, and it is best that I fade into the ether as far as she knows. She probably hasn't had a second thought about me, anyway.

When I was in town last month, I found myself looking for any sign of her everywhere I went. I wouldn't allow myself to ride by the house. Olivier had a Rolls Royce that week, which would have stuck out like a sore thumb.

I am so ashamed of how I behaved that I don't think I want to run into her. I just don't know why I can shake her.

I make a decision to take a trip out there. I need to check on the Virginia Beach project anyway. I was approached about buying another three hundred acres adjacent to our development. This is a perfect time to walk that dirt and start the negotiations so we can rework the master-planned urban development plan.

I have my last mediation meeting today for the Claire Stackhouse debacle. I couldn't bring myself to bend over and take it up the ass from her anymore. So, against my attorney's advice, I pushed back.

Based on our conversation that night, I have a sneaking suspicion that that would have been Hollis's advice.

I didn't agree to the original offer she made to drop the case against her for stealing my beach house in exchange for her dropping the sexual harassment claims. She was trying to take advantage of me again, so I called her bluff.

After months of going back and forth, she agreed to recant her sexual harassment accusations. She pleaded guilty to a lesser charge of trespassing in exchange for the DA dropping the more serious fraud charges.

It has been a bitch living under the shadow of Claire's accusations. In today's world, just an accusation is enough to put someone under. I can hear the whispers every now and then still. The further we get away from it, and with no noise except for the initial few weeks in March, the less it seems to be a part of our culture here at the office or in the field. But I doubt I will ever completely clean that off of my name.

I would be lying if I said it didn't affect me. I wish I could be better at letting things like that roll off my back. There should be some real repercussions for people making false character assassinations. Unfortunately, there just aren't. If someone has thick skin, a dead heart, and an understanding of how to game the system, kings can be brought to their knees—all over lies.

I digress.

I pick up the phone on my desk and buzz Everly's desk.

"Hello?"

"Everly, will you please set up a meeting with Thomas Earhardt? I want to fly east to meet with him and discuss the extra three hundred acres. I'd say in the next few days if he is available."

"Yessir, I am on it. Will you stay in Virginia Beach or NC?"

"I'll be staying in Duck, so please also make sure the house is clean and that Olivier can meet me at the airport. Let me know once all of that is set up and my travel dates."

"Will do."

I make the decision, allowing a wave of calm to wash over me. I have been in knots since this morning, and making this call gives me a sense of peace about the whole thing. In all likelihood, I won't see her, but something about just going there makes me feel like I am doing something.

The mere thought of the possibility of reencountering her fills my heart with an additional snippet of hope. I don't plan to see her, nor will I be involved in the renovation, but something inside of me hopes our paths cross again so that I can apologize for the way I left in March.

The phone is still in my hand after my conversation with Everly when it buzzes. I look at it, and time stops when I see her name.

> Thanks, Grayson. I appreciate it. I'm sorry for your sweet house, but luckily seems like most of it can be salvaged. Hope you're well.

TWENTY

Hollis
———————

2:38 pm EST

MY HEART IS JUST NOW COMING down from the simple, innocuous text reply I sent to Grayson several minutes ago.

You'd think I told him I was awaiting his son's arrival any minute with how much I toiled over sending the text. But I wanted to be better than him. I didn't want to ignore his text, so I replied. And I left out the most important news I should have shared with him.

As I wait for the resident to return, I scroll through Instagram, looking at all the perfect lives in my social sphere. I am in one of the deepest valleys of my life - my house just burned down, I am sitting in the E.R. alone, and I am about to become a single mom. Things couldn't possibly be any worse. Looking at the perfectly curated posts by my friends and their happy lives seems like an excellent idea at the moment.

My phone rings. It is Everly, the property manager. She has been very attentive and on it as soon as I called her at what was the butt-crack of dawn on the west coast this morning to let her know about the fire.

When she asked if I wanted to stay if they could get everything fixed, I said absolutely without skipping a beat. I was so worried that the fire would essentially mean the end of my Duck Dynasty and that I would be moving back to Virginia to live with my parents, another low blow to my already dismal prospects in life.

"Hello," I say into the phone, hoping this heart rate monitor beeping isn't detectable over the phone.

"Hi, Ms. Mitchell. This is Everly. I have reserved a suite for you at the Sanderling until we can repair your house. I have already coordinated someone to come in and pack up all of your things. Are you able to meet him today at 5:30 to see if any of the damaged things can be salvaged?"

"Thank you so much. Sure, I think I can be there then."

I have nothing else to do, I think to myself, except finish my novel that has already gone over my editor's deadline, buy a car seat for the new baby, and, oh, have a baby.

"Great. They will start then and work until everything is packed or discarded from the home. The contractor says we should be done with the whole renovation in ten weeks, at which time the movers will move your things back in."

I am blown away by all they are doing to soften this blow. I had no idea how I would navigate this with this baby coming and the holidays coming up. Tears well in my eyes. For the tenth time today.

"The reservation will be under your name, and all incidentals will be covered for you while you are there."

We hang up, my head absorbing what all of this means. I guess I should be happy that I will not have to ask Kendall if I can shack up with her with my dog and my newborn. My parents don't even know about any of this yet.

That reminds me, I need to call my mom. She is planning to come next week and stay with me to get ready for and welcome the baby for a couple of weeks. We are planning to have our own mini-Thanksgiving.

That may change now that I am homeless. Unless she can stomach staying with me at the hotel.

We can all praise the heavens above that I will not have to move back in with the parentals for the interim. Living in a hotel feels like a pretty shitty but still better alternative, though. It isn't the warm and nesting experience I hoped to come home to either.

"Find the silver linings, Hollis. It's all we got."

I hear a slight knock on the door and am jolted out of my pity party. The smokey glass door slides open. All the doors slide open and closed automatically, so there is no slipping into a room here undetected. The familiar face of the resident, who doesn't look a day older than sixteen, walks in. He is smiling, so I am assuming the ultrasound checked out.

"Everything is stable, and the baby is happy and healthy. You are dilated five centimeters. I know you said your water hasn't broken, but I think this baby is coming in the next day or so."

For the second time today, everything is spinning. I am not ready for this. Not today. I am not due for another two weeks. I am supposed to have another week to procrastinate and figure out how I am going to do this.

"Oh, wow. I didn't realize that. I have been having what I thought were Braxton Hicks, but maybe they were real contractions. Okay." I pause. He lets the silence linger, probably at a loss for words, too. "Okay. Thank you."

He thinks I'm an idiot. I am an idiot. What made me think I could do this by myself? What kind of person am I to make this decision without talking to the father? Without even letting Grayson Sterling know that he has a child on the way?

5:01 PM *EST*

"WHY DID you leave the hospital if you are in labor?!" Kendal asks me when she sits down with me in the booth at Sacred Grounds.

"I'm not technically in labor. He just said I am dilated, and I will probably go *into* labor. Soon. I needed to get some things together. I don't even have any things anymore. At 5:30, I need to go by the house to meet the packers.

The weight of it all is heavier than my full belly. My chest is tight, and I am finding it difficult to get enough oxygen into my lungs. This can't be good for the baby.

"I don't know. I couldn't stay put in that place. Since I was in the ER, I would have had to leave anyway. There is no labor and delivery there. Just stop asking me. I am over-whelmed enough."

Kendall takes my hand and holds it between her two. "Will you go with me to my house?" I ask her. I put too much on this poor woman.

By now, I am crying audibly, no longer trying to hide it. Right here in the Sacred Grounds, still wearing my slippers. A gigantic pregnant, grown lady in slippers boohooing in front of God knows who.

Kendall pulls me to her and hugs me tight. She is getting off now and agrees to come with me to meet the packers. She stated emphatically that we would drive over to my house, though not walk. It is less than a mile, but she insisted we drive so the baby doesn't plop out on the walk there or back.

I feel bad for Kendall that she has had to be my everything these last few months. Well, nine months, to be exact. Between her and my best friend, Ava, who lives in Atlanta, I have been propped up more times than I care to remember by these precious ladies on days when I didn't think I could muscle through to another day.

Ava couldn't be here to physically pick me up off of the floor when I found out I was pregnant in April, so Kendall got the unenviable job of being my rock during those dark weeks directly after finding out. We had already become close because of my daily visits for my coffee and to write in the front booth, but going through that with me brought us even closer. These two women have been my lifeline in what has turned out to be a rocky and tumultuous 2024.

I wasn't supposed to be able to get pregnant. That is what I thought, anyway. So, I didn't bother worrying about protection the one night that Grayson and I hooked up. It all happened so fast, and it was so late. Not to mention, my body was making decisions without checking in with my head anyway.

I just never even imagined in my wildest dreams, or night-mares, that this would even be a possibility. The day my divorce becomes final, the divorce from my ex-husband with whom I could not get pregnant for years, I hook up with a complete stranger and get knocked up. Talk about a clusterfuck of colossal proportions.

Grayson left that morning after, barely offering a smile after we had slept together, refusing even to eat a piece of non-burnt toast that I had made for him. And I haven't heard a thing from him since. What was I supposed to do? Text him that I was having his baby five weeks later when I found out?

My feeble attempt at asking him to coffee a week after I got the positive pregnancy test was pathetic.

I contemplated it when he didn't respond to my attempt to tell him. Just to stick it to him.

I wasn't about to set myself up for that rejection again.

"You've got this, Hollis. We have talked about this. You are strong. And you are going to be an amazing mom. We are your village and will be there for you and sweet baby Reeves. He is already so loved, just like his momma."

"You're an amazing friend. I don't know what I would do without you. Thank you. I'm hoping Reeves' stuff isn't ruined by the water. Otherwise, I have nothing for him if he comes tonight."

"We will make sure he has something. Regardless. But yes, let's get over there and see what we can get for you two. And then let's go to my house for some hot tea and wait for this baby boy to decide to join us. Preferably after we leave your house."

TWENTY-ONE

Grayson

Norfolk International Airport

Thursday, December 5th

· 1:26 *pm EST / 10:26 am PST*

I HEAR and feel the wheels drop, the familiar thump letting me know we are close to Norfolk International. Right on schedule. I open the shade at the window beside me. My mind wanders to the sleepy town as I peer out the window at the sprawling expanse of the coastal landscape below.

My adrenaline should be pumping about adding to what is slated to be one of the most significant and most successful developments on the East Coast. Instead, it couldn't be further from my mind.

"Welcome to Norfolk International Airport," a familiar voice says over the speaker as the plane taxis toward the gate. I always request Taylor to be the flight attendant when we fly. She knows what I need even before I do.

After taxiing and stopping at the private hangar, Taylor comes by one last time to ensure I need nothing else. We have this down. Another benchmark, telling me I can get off the plane now.

The other attendant starts unlocking the door, disengaging the steps down. I spot Olivier's black Suburban parked on the other side of the chain link fence, ready and waiting, as it should be.

I thank her and reply, "No, I'm all set." She and the rest of the crew will stay nearby tonight as we are scheduled to fly back out tomorrow afternoon.

As I descend the steps to the tarmac, my thoughts wander back to Hollis and the house fire. Thanksgiving is next week, and I wonder if she will stay at the resort or head out of town to be with family. She doesn't have her home because of the fire. My fire.

Olivier meets me at the bottom of the steps. We exchange pleasantries as he gets my hanging bag and roller board from the crew member, and we head toward the car.

"Good to see you, Mr. Grayson. How was your flight?" Olivier inquires warmly, more chipper than usual. I force a smile.

"It was smooth, Olivier. Thanks for being here," I reply. My preoccupation remains.

As we make our way toward Virginia Beach for my meeting with Thomas, my emotions are fucking all over the place. The excitement of the project and the angst over the pressing concerns for Hollis and her home are at odds and strangely affecting me.

I look out of the window to try to take my mind off everything. The roads are in excellent condition, offering a smooth and efficient journey. I find comfort in the familiar hum of the car's engine and the occasional knee-tapping song on the radio. I should be reviewing the Letter of Intent and the survey, but I have no desire to look at any of it. Instead, I stare out of the window.

The drive to Virginia Beach takes about half an hour. As we arrive at Thomas's office, I step out of the car and walk into the building while Olivier drives off and parks nearby. The reception area is sleek and professional, with contemporary artwork adorning the walls. The muted tones and modern furnishings feel clean and professional. The soft-spoken receptionist welcomes me with a polite smile as she announces my arrival.

"Good afternoon, Mr. Sterling. How was your flight in?"

"It was nice, thank you." Sometimes, these necessary evils of small talk grate on me more than others. She means no harm. This is her job, but I have no inclination to talk to her. So, I offer nothing more than a short answer to her question that she likely has no desire to know the answer to.

"Mr. Earhardt is expecting you. I'll let him know you are coming up."

"Thanks so much," I say to her as I walk away toward the elevators.

Thomas's office, located on the top floor, offers a panoramic view of the city, the coastline stretching out in the distance. The spacious, well-appointed room exudes an air of authority and success.

Thomas has done well for himself. He isn't in the realm of development that I am, but then again, not many are. But he has made some outstanding contributions to the state of Virginia and the Eastern Coast all the way down to South Carolina.

The polished wooden desk, the array of awards and accolades, and the floor-to-ceiling windows framing the ocean view showcase his success. He should be proud of all he has done. I know I am indeed grateful that he reached out to me and asked me to partner with him on this. I have the capital, and he has the connections. Doing this as an outsider alone would have been nearly impossible.

———

DUCK, *NC*

8:17 pm EST

I LEFT my office early this morning, making my way to the airport at the ass crack of dawn. I caught a flight to the East Coast, followed by a drive to Virginia Beach for my meeting with Thomas. When I finally get to Duck, my body immediately relaxes.

After an exhaustive day that has taken me across three different states, I open the door and drink in the familiar and comforting smell unique to my beach house.

I step out onto the deck. The gentle sound of waves crashing on the shore provides a soothing end to the long day. It is this, these moments, that I work so tirelessly for, what I live for.

The night sky stretches above me, a canopy of stars that glistens like so many diamonds, and the salty scent of the sea hangs in the air. This is where I feel most comfortable and most able to relax. It's too bad I am only here for one night. One of these days, I will start spending most of my time here. One day.

As I stand on the deck, memories of that first night I met Hollis come flooding back, a vivid and bittersweet recollection. Being here now always reminds me of her. I recall how her eyes lit up as we talked and our strong and undeniable connection.

The world felt as if it belonged to just the two of us. I remember her words, her dreams, and the genuine laughter that flowed freely, unburdened by the constraints of the outside world.

Since that night, I have constantly wished I had handled things differently. It's a vacuum that seems to have grown since that morning that I left in haste. As I stand here on the deck, gazing at the night sky and listening to the waves, it's impossible not to wonder what could have been.

I am having a hard time grasping the feelings I have for her. I think I want to get closer to her. This feeling is foreign to me. My heart aches with the memories of a connection that remains suspended in time.

As much as I want to deny it, I wanted to come here for the primary reason to be close to her. I won't see or talk to her, but knowing she is nearby gives me pause.

FRIDAY, *December 6th*

2:22 am EST

"I WAS HOPING I would run into you here."

"Well, it is quite a surprise to see you. I wish you had told me you were in town. I had no idea you were into book readings."

"I didn't know I was until I saw you reading that chapter. I can't believe what I have been missing my whole life. You are so fucking sexy I could barely sit there until you were done."

I feel myself grow inside of my pants as I say this. She licks her lips, her tongue pausing and moving dramatically slowly. My insides are on fire. Why is she doing this to me?

She lets out a moan and leans her body into mine. Her eyes are closed as her head is tilted up to mine. She presses her midsection into mine, letting me know that we are still very much into each other.

I was nervous before coming, not sure how I would be received. Seeing her up there tonight reading, her voice sultry and self-assured, I knew I couldn't let this time slip by without trying to make amends for the last time.

"I haven't stopped thinking about you," I whisper into her ear, my warm breath ricocheting off her skin back to my mouth.

She grabs my hand and pulls me. She leads me down a dimly lit hallway. This feels nothing like any bookstore I have ever been in.

There is a door to the right. She looks up and down the hall, appearing to make sure no one sees us, and then she opens the door quickly, pulling me in with her.

It is an oversized closet full of boxes and books. There is a window, and the light from a street lamp lights the room only slightly. Just enough to highlight Hollis. Her face is bathed in the outline, backlit from the window.

She pulls me down to her face, placing her lips on mine. She thrusts her tongue into my mouth, drawing me in.

Her hand reaches down and cups my engorged dick, rubbing it. She is teasing me, challenging me. I reach down and, take off my belt and unfasten my pants, letting her do the rest. She pulls my pants down, putting her hand inside of my boxers, teasing me further.

I let out a moan, utterly untethered from all reality. I turn us around and press her against the closed door. I lift her dress over her head, revealing her completely naked, perfect body. She has no bra or underwear on.

I jerk my boxers down as she spreads her legs, ready for me. I plunge myself into her, lifting her onto my hips.

She straddles me, and I thrust myself deeper into her, and she comes immediately. Using the door as leverage, I gyrate faster than I have ever moved, wanting more and more of her. Her wet, tight body on my shaft makes me come faster than I would like. But the primal need won't allow me to stop or slow down.

I explode inside of her, pressing into her until I stop pulsing. Our sweaty bodies are entangled, tied. I inhale her scent, absorbing all of her into me.

When I open my eyes, we are on the stage, and everyone in the audience is watching us. I feel the need to immediately shield her, wanting to protect her from prying eyes. She laughs when she sees my panic, causing me to cover myself.

The joke is on me.

I jolt upright and realize I am in my bed, not in a bookstore, making love to Hollis. I am soaking wet, having ejaculated in my bed.

I feel warmth for having the opportunity to see her again and deflated once the realization hits me that it wasn't real.

I get out of bed to clean myself up. How have I let this woman get in my head like this? This house is filled with her spirit. Knowing she is just down the street has brought her even more to the forefront of my mind.

After I shower I walk downstairs to sleep in the guest room we shared that fateful night. I climb in and feel such an emptiness, knowing she is so close, but I might as well be in California.

———

7:19 *am EST*

ON OUR WAY out of town, Olivier pulls the sleek, black SUV into a spot near the Sacred Grounds coffee shop. Time is tight this morning, but I need another coffee.

I'm flying straight to a crucial meeting in San Diego, so I'm dressed in my three-piece suit. The heels of my loafers are loud on the wood floor, announcing my exit just as they did for my entrance.

The casual atmosphere inside the coffee shop makes me feel a tad out of place. As usual, I don't blend in among the beach-casual crowd, but that doesn't bother me anymore now than ever. I glance around while I wait in line, taking in the cozy interior with its exposed brick walls, mismatched wooden furniture, and the rich aroma of freshly brewed coffee filling the air.

As I walk back towards the door with my large coffee in hand, I spot a large golden retriever lounging on the worn wood floor to my right, just before the door.

Mr. Bojangles! Mixed emotions wash over me. Bending down, I pet the dog, feeling a stirring deep down inside of me. I look around, hoping to see Hollis, but she's nowhere in sight. My heart sinks. Somehow, the simple act of petting the dog, once an object of my disdain, excites me. Knowing that he is part of her gives me a connection I have yearned for.

My cottage, Hollis's house, is two blocks from here on the way out of town. I ask Olivier to drive that route instead of getting back on the causeway. I tell myself that it is to check out the damage.

But really, I am hoping to steal a glance of her walking to or from the café.

Fucking A. I'm unprepared for what I see. The charred roof is partially gone, and the telltale signs of smoke damage mar the front elevation of the house. The sight of the ruins leaves me distraught and upset. I tell Olivier to keep driving, not to stop.

Suddenly, I am nauseous.

The once-charming home, now a shell of its former self, is a painful reminder of the fire that disrupted Hollis's life.

We head to Norfolk International Airport, the early morning sun casting a gray, cold pallor across the sky. The contrast between the golden retriever's warmth and the devastation at Hollis's house lingers in my mind, making the ride to the airport feel much longer than it is.

TWENTY-TWO

Hollis

Tuesday, August 18th, 2020

8:14 *am EST*

IT'S hard to believe my baby boy is nine months old today. Time has flown by, yet most of my days feel never-ending. Reeves keeps me on my toes, that is for sure.

So many times, I have wanted to share his milestones with Grayson. To send him a cute picture I snapped of him laughing or when he cut his first tooth. Or the time he smeared blueberries all over his face and was so proud of himself.

With the pandemic this year, everything has been weird. But having all of this time just the two of us has been amazing. I've often wondered that Grayson is doing or how he is getting through this insane world.

Having Reeves helps me put all of the noise outside of my brain. We live in our bubble and that is just fine by me.

I see so much of Grayson in him.

He's grown so much. He is pulling himself up and cruising along furniture, his tiny feet taking the occasional independent step before he plops down with a cheerful grin. Reeves is a bright and happy baby, and I've often heard people comment on how he seems like an old soul, so focused and intense.

Life as a new mom, especially as a single mom, has been a hurricane of challenges and joys. Raising Reeves without any help has been daunting at times, but it's also been incredibly rewarding. The love I feel for him is immeasurable.

These past two years have been tumultuous, but they've also provided me with a wealth of material for my books. In fact, I've had two books hit the New York Times #1 bestsellers list, and the financial stability they've brought has allowed me to provide for Reeves comfortably.

Still, there are moments when I can't help but wonder what life might have been like if things had turned out differently with Grayson. I see expressions on Reeves's face that remind me of expressions he made that night. While I don't dwell on it every day as I did throughout my pregnancy, the thoughts are never too far away.

What if Grayson had been more receptive to me that next morning? What if we'd been dating or at least in contact when I found out I was pregnant? Would we have made the decisions together? Would he be in Reeves' life now? The hypotheticals linger in the background, overshadowed by the reality of my current life.

I haven't met or dated anyone since Reeves was born, and the thought of it barely crosses my mind. My days are already too full between writing and taking care of him. We don't even get to visit Sacred Grounds as often as we used to, but sometimes I bring Reeves with me. He's usually bundled up in his baby Bjorn, snuggled up to me as we venture out into the world.

My life is a quiet existence where the world mainly revolves around my baby. I don't mind it, though. I am grateful to have so much time to be with him and watch him grow. I swear he does something new daily, and I get to be here for it all.

My family has been incredible, offering their support and love from afar. They're so far away, and my parents stay so busy that I don't get to see them as often as I'd like. It's Kendall who's been my rock, my steadfast friend who has stepped in to fill the gaps when I need that extra pair of hands or a sympathetic ear. She is, without a doubt, Reeves' surrogate second parent.

As Reeves grows, I find solace in the fact that I've finally emerged from the sleepless nights and constant crying that defined his first several months. He now sleeps through the night, and I've never been so grateful to go to bed at sunset and sleep through the night. Motherhood has been a revelation, and despite the challenges, I wouldn't change a thing.

Learning that Grayson was in the coffee shop just before Thanksgiving last year hits me like a tidal wave of emotions. Kendall saw him, recognized him immediately, and her words cut through me like a razor.

She told me how he bent down to pet Mr. Bojangles and then, quite obviously, scanned the room, searching for me. It's a moment frozen in time and one I can't help but replay in my mind over and over.

Ever the gentle proponent, Kendall encouraged me to reach out to him to seize the opportunity to reconnect. But I couldn't bring myself to do it. We texted a little after the fire, but I haven't heard from him since. And what was I supposed to say, "Hey! I heard you were in town. Guess what? You're a dad!"

That week, I was out of town, staying with my family in Virginia while Kendall looked after Mr. Bojangles. The thought of traveling with a new baby and a dog felt insurmountable, and while I hated to leave him, I knew he was in good hands with Kendall. The weight of not being there, of missing that moment when Grayson and Reeves could have crossed paths, is something I can't shake.

I have thought about it a hundred times since she told me. How would that have gone? Would he have recognized Reeves as his own? Would he have done the math and connected the dots? What would we have talked about?

TWENTY-THREE

Grayson

Norfolk International Airport

Friday, August 11th, 2023

4:44 PM *EST*

MY LIFE HAS BEEN a tornado lately, with work demanding every ounce of my attention. The prospect of two weeks at my beach house is a welcome escape from the relentless pace of my professional life. I will have some work here, but I plan to try to take most of the time to decompress and reset.

I just broke up with Blanca, my girlfriend of almost two years. And it feels incredible.

The plane touches down smoothly. I gather my belongings, eager to embark on this much-needed break. The drive from the airport is always too long. Especially coming from the West Coast, I am ready to be there after three hours in the air. But the lush greenery and coastal vistas always bring me a sense of calm.

As we make our way, I am eager about the upcoming ribbon-cutting event for the new mixed-use development in Virginia Beach. The Harbor Vista project is a culmination of hard work and dedication. I look forward to celebrating its completion with the community.

It has been a long and often intense eight years in the making. The development is a testament to the vision and effort that has gone into transforming this area. To say that I am proud of our achievements is a significant under-statement.

Blanca and I had our fun together, but the relationship ran its course. In the end, there was no real spark, no deep connection. The decision to break up was right, but it's still an adjustment.

She was supposed to be with me for the Harbor Vista ribbon cutting. It is strange to be going alone, such a big project. But I am still looking forward to it, regardless.

Closing in on forty, I am at peace being alone. I've always been okay with only myself to rely on.

I'm met with a sense of solitude that's both peaceful and unnerving. I don't miss Blanca. She had a more chal-lenging time with it, but I remain resolute in my choice. The truth is, we were never truly in love, never truly connected on a deeper level. The relationship had become more of a comfortable habit than a true bond.

As I enter the house, the sweeping view of the Atlantic Ocean stretches before me, the warm welcome I always look forward to. I take a deep breath and drink in my safe space.

I glance over to the fireplace and see in my mind's eye Hollis sitting there with her hands wrapped around her mug, laughing about something. I haven't thought about her as much as I did at first, but I still think about her. In fact, how I remember her and our time together is part of the reason I knew I couldn't be with Bianca. I'd never had those deep, visceral feelings about her.

"I will take your bags up to your room, Mr. Grayson, if that is okay?"

I'm snapped out of my head at the sound of Olivier's voice.

"Yes, of course. Thank you, Olivier."

He will be staying at The Sanderling. It is a bit of a vacation for him, too, because I won't be doing too much driving. The trip to Virginia for the grand reveal for Harbor Vista is the only definite trip on the books. And then, of course, dinner a few times at Cafe Pamlico.

The sound of the waves crashing against the shore and the salty scent of the sea fill me.

A haunting question resurfaces whenever I find myself in the Outer Banks: Why haven't I reached out to her since the fire? Hollis. The answer, I suppose, is more complex than I'd like to admit.

The memories of that night are shrouded in the heady mix of desire, hope, and a sense of connection that I've never quite felt before. And, although I know our paths diverged after that night, the feeling of unfinished business lingers.

The passing of time has not dulled the sharpness of the memory, nor has it eased the ache that gnaws at my heart when I think of her. I tell myself it's because I'm focused on my work, that we live on opposite ends of the country, that I need to maintain my independence.

But the truth is, deep down, I know that the thought of reaching out to her is tempered by the fear of rejection and my aversion to complicating her life. Her simple, uncomplicated life doesn't want to be injected with the chaos my busy life would bring.

TWENTY-FOUR

Hollis

Saturday, August 12th

9:37 am EST

REEVES HAS BEEN OBSESSED with the ocean and the beach lately. Since the summer is slipping away, we go whenever there is a beautiful day. We are there pretty much every day, building sandcastles, walking Mr. Bojangles, and splashing in the surf. Watching the world through his eyes has been the greatest gift of my life.

The early morning sun hangs low on the horizon, casting a warm, golden glow over the nearly deserted beach as we wind down the summer. This is my favorite time of the year here. Not yet cold, but for the most part, it is a ghost town. We have the beach to ourselves.

With most vacationers returning to the rhythms of school and everyday life, the shoreline is blissfully empty, save for the occasional passerby. An older man, about 30 yards up the beach, is engrossed in his morning fishing, his silhouette a solitary figure against the vast expanse of sea and sand.

I park my bike at the beach access, lift Reeves out of the bike seat, and we head down. I unfasten Mr. Bojangles' leash from his collar, letting him run ahead of us. He heads straight to the small shore birds feasting on something.

As Reeves and I take our first steps onto the egress on the dune, the warm sand instantly relaxes me. I am in my happy place.

The warm, gentle breeze caresses my skin. The air is thick with the promise of another sun-kissed morning, and I can't help but smile as I finally feel that we have reached a flow of peace and contentment in our life.

Reeves is already running ahead, his tiny footprints imprinting a trail toward the water. His laughter and joy are everything I live for.

He pauses every now and then to pick up a seashell, eyes wide with wonder as he examines each one in the soft morning light. To him, each shell is a treasure, and he presents them to me with the kind of pure excitement only a four-year-old can muster.

I squat down beside him. He is inspecting a dinosaur-looking horseshoe crab carcass.

"What dis?" He asks, pointing.

"That is called a horseshoe crab. Do you want to touch his shell? He won't mind. Just do it gently. See these points? They could hurt you if you're not careful."

He cautiously touches the shiny side of the shell with his left hand and pulls it back quickly. It is looking like he will be a lefty, which I adore. Every little unique thing that makes him Reeves warms my heart.

The wet sand is noticeably cooler than the dry, soft sand was when we walked down. It is slightly damp beneath my toes, a refreshing contrast to the warmth of the air. A slight chill travels through me.

Once the horseshoe crab is no longer a novel find, Reeves is off. I watch as he picks up a handful of sand at the shoreline and lets it slip through his fingers, the grains running like tiny rivers back to their rightful place. He giggles and does it again, delighting in the simple pleasure of this repetitive act.

The water's edge is a mirror, reflecting the soft blue of the sky above. I dip my toes into the water, feeling its cool embrace. Reeves, noticing the change in temperature, takes my other hand. His tiny feet splash through the shallows as he squeals with the thrill of the waves gently tickling as they lick his toes and then roll back out to sea.

The beach is a place of solace, a sanctuary where I've found my place. Despite the trials and tribulations that life has thrown my way, I feel fulfilled and settled here. The happiness I've found in my role as a mother is unparalleled. As I watch Reeves, his laughter and innocent curiosity shaping the world around him, my heart swells with a profound sense of love and contentment.

In this moment, with the sun on our faces and the gentle waves at our feet, I am grateful for this serene slice of life. The beach, Reeves, and the simple joys surrounding us have allowed me to find my place of belonging and my corner of happiness. This beach, this precious time spent with my son, reflects the peace I've yearned for and finally found.

I stand up to stretch my back after bending down looking for shark's teeth. I notice a man walking down the beach towards us. Something about him stirs a sense of déjà vu deep within me.

I can't help but keep looking up, my gaze intermittently drawn to him. I can't make out his distinct features, but I can tell he's remarkably handsome. Tall, with light brown hair, his physique is undeniably fit, and his strong shoulders are accentuated by how he carries himself.

He's dressed in khakis and a crisp white button-down shirt, the sleeves casually rolled up, as if he's emerged straight from the pages of a beachside fashion catalog.

As he draws nearer, my heart flutters with an unidentifiable recognition.

As the man gets closer, his face comes into sharper focus, and it suddenly hits me like a tidal wave. It's Grayson Sterling.

Blissfully oblivious to my inner disarray, Reeves continues to build drip castles, his laughter echoing through the salty breeze. I steal glances at the approaching man between moments spent watching my son's pure joy and wonderment at every broken shell and fiddler crab.

I don't know if I should acknowledge him or look down and let us both avoid an awkward exchange. What if he recognizes himself in Reeves?!

My heart, fluttering with uncertainty, now thunders in my chest, a wild storm of emotions churning within me. I haven't seen him in over four years and never thought I would cross paths with him again.

My body reacts to the sudden revelation. My palms grow clammy, and my breath catches in my throat. The years that have passed between us and the guilt I've harbored for not telling him about Reeves come crashing down upon me. It's as if time has stood still, and the weight of it covers me like a wet quilt, making it hard for me to breathe.

The million thoughts that race through my mind are a clamor of doubt, regret, and fear of what he might think. Will he recognize me after all these years? Will he notice the uncanny resemblance between Reeves and himself?

Should I stop him to say hi, to explain, to apologize?

Should I grab Mr. Bojangles and Reeves and run?

I wish I had some sort of lifeline, a "phone a friend" to guide me through this moment, to tell me what the right thing to do is.

TWENTY-FIVE

Grayson

10:02 am EST

MY NEW LEASE on life includes cussing less and taking time to appreciate all that I work for. And that starts with my extended vacation here at my favorite spot on the planet. And morning walks.

I spot a woman and her young child up ahead, and I immediately know. It's Hollis. If I hadn't recognized her, Mr. Bojangles, who is not far from her side, would have been a dead giveaway. The sight of her, after all of this time, floods me with a combination of excitement and nervousness. My pace quickens, and I can feel the adrenaline coursing through my veins.

The beach seems to stretch on forever, the sand underfoot cool and soft, the sound of the waves constant in their rhythmic ebb and flow on the shore. I want to be there near her and simultaneously turn and walk the other way.

I have wished I had done things differently a thousand times. I have begged the universe for a do-over. Now is my chance. I will finally have at least the opportunity to look into her eyes again.

The brilliant sunshine bathes the scene in a soft, golden light as if nature itself is conspiring to make this reunion happen. My senses are heightened, every detail of the moment in clear focus.

Seeing Hollis, Mr. Bojangles and who I can only assume is her son, hits me in the gut. The universe is showing me that I missed the boat on this one. Married with a family is the rite of passage that most of my friends our age are experiencing, and as usual, I am on the outside looking in. Wondering if she is the one I let get away.

I'm not sure what I should do or say, but the undeniable connection we once shared surges through me, and I can't help but think I have to say something. We are connected, if by nothing else, by the fact that she lives in my rental.

My heart pounds in my chest as I approach.

My pace quickens, anxious to say something, anything. I take in the details of the scene. Beautiful and radiant, Hollis stands near the shore, her child sitting and digging in the sand.

As I draw closer, her features now entirely in focus, it becomes evident that Hollis recognizes me, too. Our eyes meet, and in that unspoken moment, it is evident the connection between us is still there. My heart skips a beat, and a rush of warmth surges through my body, making my skin prickle.

My voice, betraying my nervousness, trembles as I offer a soft, "Hollis?" It is stated as a question, but there is no doubt in my mind who she is. The single word hangs in the air, carrying the weight of all the years that have passed since our last encounter.

As we lock eyes, I can't help but notice how time has treated her with kindness. She's just as beautiful as I remember, her eyes sparkling with a hint of mischief and an air of quiet strength. The waves of her brown hair, with golden strands kissed by the sun, frame her face. Her smile, though tentative, is still as enchanting as ever. Motherhood suits her.

The beachside meeting is filled with unspoken words and unanswered questions. The gravity of it all is like a silent weight pressing down on my shoulders. There's a sense of vulnerability in this moment as we stand on the same sand, once again connected by fate. I am a different man than I was five years ago.

Though I'm uncertain about what this means for me, there's no doubt that Hollis's presence has rekindled something within me that I've long tried to bury. Feelings I have been attempting to deny, to escape, to push down. Seeing her again, everything comes rushing to the surface.

"Grayson," she says, her voice carrying an air of astonishment and a hint of emotion. A large smile on her face puts any fear I had about how things ended out of my mind. The sound of my name on her lips fills me with warmth.

"Wow. I can't believe it is you! How the heck are you?" She asks, confident and disarming. Her natural beauty is stunning, the quiet beach a perfect backdrop.

We exchange pleasantries, sharing the standard inquiries about life and what has transpired since we last saw each other.

She introduces me to her son, a lively, spirited little boy. He flashes a mischievous grin when she says, "Reeves, this is Grayson." In the blink of an eye, he's off and running, the vast beach stretching out before him like a playground of endless possibility.

I notice she doesn't have a ring on her left hand, leaving a thread of possibility that she isn't married.

I hang onto our easy banter, not wanting to continue my journey to nowhere. I have transitioned from quick small talk to digging into a more substantial conversation. "I am so sorry about the fire in your house. How are the renovations for you? Are you happy with the house?"

"Oh, yeah. That was a doozy. But I am so grateful for the way it went down. I went into labor with him," she says as she points to Reeves. "It felt like the worst timing, but I will say, living at The Sanderling those first two months with him ended up being a blessing in disguise. Thank you for taking care of everything like you did. Everly is amazing, by the way. She is very easy to work with."

"She is great. I am so glad you're happy with everything. I have felt so terrible about it all."

I so badly want to apologize for how I left things. It feels silly at this point. It was probably a blip in her world, and I doubt she even thought about it again. Again, a missed opportunity. I should have been more forthcoming then. I should be braver now.

TWENTY-SIX

Hollis

11:11 am EST

SEEING Grayson again this morning brings up a whirlwind of emotions. It is hitting me more deeply than I even imagined at this point it would. Five years later, he still has this hold on me.

And the guilt. The guilt grips me. Out of sight, out of mind never resonated more than it does right now. Because in sight is putting everything top of mind.

As I looked into those familiar, deep blue eyes and the strong lines of his face, memories of that night we spent together came flooding back. It was as if time flipped backward, and I was transported back to that unforgettable evening.

For me, our conversation is a little like walking through a minefield, a combination of getting to know each other again and navigating the unspoken heaviness that exists between us. The weight of which only I am aware of.

It's a strange juxtaposition. We had such an intimate experience and are linked through the rental, but we don't know each other at all. A stronger bond interconnects us, but he doesn't know that.

I wondered if he would even recognize me, but I never imagined he would stand here with us and talk for almost an hour. The last time we met, he barely had time to stop and enjoy his own home, much less chat with a stranger. Oddly, now he seems to have all the time in the world.

My mind is so present with him, talking, that I lose track of time. Suddenly it occurs to me that my mom is probably already at my house, waiting to pick up Reeves.

"I am so sorry, but I am going to have to run. My mom is probably at my house, alerting all the neighbors that we are missing. Reeves is going to stay with my parents for a week, and I know she is wondering where we are."

"No worries at all. I am sorry I have hijacked your quiet morning. It was so nice to run into you and meet your son. And see this big guy," he says as he bends down to pet Mr. Bojangles. Wow, he has softened in the few years since we have seen each other.

Without thinking about the last time I put myself out there and made him breakfast, I blurted out, "Would you like to see the house? It's been several years now, but the new kitchen and back patio since the fire are a nice change from before. It makes for a more logical use of the space when we flipped the kitchen to the other side, making room for an actual dining space."

I feel dumb for even suggesting it. He is probably so far removed from this that he doesn't know or care. Oh, well. There is no harm in throwing it out there.

"I would love that. I wanted to ask you a few times that I have been in town but didn't want to intrude. But I would love to see what you guys have done with the place."

"You want to come by in an hour or so?"

I almost invited him to walk back with us, but I can't deal with the looks I know my mom will give me. It will take her all of two seconds to see the resemblance, and her internal dialogue is delayed. There is no telling what she might say.

"That sounds great. Are you sure that isn't an imposition on you?"

"Not an imposition at all. My mom and Reeves will be gone by then, so you won't have to deal with Crazy Roberta," I say with a laugh. That is the nickname my friends and I gave my mom in high school because she is like a Tasmanian Devil, always running around like a chicken with her head cut off.

"I hate to run so abruptly, but she is probably there, so I will see you at the house in about an hour?"

The gravity of our fateful night feels like an awkward albatross between us. Neither of us seems quite sure how to navigate that with the present.

Not to mention the added angst I have. Not because I hold a grudge anymore, but because he obviously hasn't made the connection. Reeves' age and his uncanny resemblance to Grayson himself do not seem to register. With his brown, wavy hair and bright blue eyes, Reeves is like a reflection of Grayson himself. How could he not see it?

12:35 PM *EST*

A GENTLE BREEZE ruffles the curtains of my cozy beachfront cottage as I sit on the back deck, drinking an iced tea. I have the windows open, bringing the outside in. Another perk of this time of the year here. It's still warm out, but not prohibitively so.

Mom and Reeves left about thirty minutes ago, and the quiet almost feels uncomfortable. Now, to figure out what to do with all of this time for the next two weeks.

I've had time to reflect on my and Grayson's unexpected encounter at the beach. He said he would come by when we parted ways. I half still believe he will show.

I expect something more important will come up, and I am fine with that. Seeing him made my whole body feel dangerously crazy. This tells me that the less I interact with him, the better. I mean, does he really ever need to know that Reeves is his son? He might want to remain oblivious if he didn't make the connection.

As if on cue, I hear a knock on the front door. My heart rate immediately speeds up, and I instinctively make sure I haven't spilled anything on my shirt and wipe invisible crumbs off my lap.

"Welcome!" I say, opening the door. I look out as he walks in, looking for a car or a driver. "Did you walk here?"

"I am trying to get out and smell the flowers more. Take more time. It seemed like a great day for a walk. Yes, I did walk here. It is closer than I thought it was."

I am speechless. That is a significant change, as he was so busy last time he couldn't even take a minute to say bye that morning. He also went on and on about being upset that he had to drive himself from the airport, ruining his morning, and talking about his "regular driver," whatever that even means.

"Oh, that is great! It is a beautiful time to walk, and it is quiet, so it is a relaxing morning on the beach. Please, come on in."

The kitchen, once modest, now boasts a touch of sophistication. New appliances and fixtures gleam in the bright natural light flowing through the house. The stone countertops exude a contemporary elegance. A significant difference from before, but the vintage charm is maintained.

As we continue the tour, I highlight other subtle enhancements: freshly painted walls and new reclaimed wood flooring. Most are similar, if not the same, to the original, but there is an updated feel throughout. I am proud of what we did and the home that Reeves and I have made here—a mirror of the transformation in my own life.

As we walk through, Grayson is generous with his compliments and seems genuinely pleased with everything. "Hollis, this place looks incredible. You guys have done an amazing job with the renovations. The kitchen, in particular, is impressive."

I smile with a sense of pride in my eyes. "Thank you, Grayson. I wanted to make it more functional and bring in some modern touches while maintaining its cozy charm."

Although our conversation is easy, I can't help but feel like a big, fat fake. The undeclared elephant in the room is stomping on my head. But for now, we focus on the house and the changes that were made. That is light and easy enough.

He keeps talking about me in the plural. Does he think that Reeves really contributes to all of this? And then it hits me. He thinks I am married.

"Thank you. I've loved this place. You might have to peel me out of here. This is home for Reeves and me." I emphasize that it is just the two of us, hopefully sending home the point that there is no one else. "Would you like to see the deck? That is the best part of the changes."

"I would love to see the deck!"

On the way out he notices my splurge, our dining table.

"This table is so neat. What is this? Is it driftwood?"

Sure enough, it is. Good eye. For a man with such attention to detail, how in the world did he miss the glaring one on the beach this morning?!

"Yes, it is. A local craftsman makes furniture out of driftwood he sources up and down the East Coast. I met him at a book release in Virginia Beach a couple of years ago, but it turns out he lives in the Outer Banks, a few towns up."

It is a thick, rough-hewn table top on four simple legs. It is well-loved by Reeves and me. We eat at this table for pretty much every meal. Reeves still sits in a booster seat in the chair on the far side, and the sphere of crumbs around it makes it apparent if the booster didn't.

Before reconfiguring the kitchen, there was no space for anything larger than a small, two-person bistro table. That would be fine for a single adult but would have made it hard for a little guy. I have spent many a meal watching him smear peas and pasta noodles wherever he could reach from his perch at this table. It is part of our story now.

"It's really neat. I will have to get his name from you. I want to have a table made for the beach house. I love it."

He seems lighter. Happier. I can't put my finger on it, but it's similar to how he was that first night. Or rather, that only night. I've since formed the opinion that the grumpy, foul-mouthed, pretentious guy I met earlier that day and experienced that morning was the real him. It is refreshing to know I was wrong.

We walk out the back door to the deck. The builder insisted on using Ipe, a Brazilian walnut hardwood, for the decking. It is a stunning wood, smoother and darker than pine. We get intense afternoon sun out here, and he said pine would require replacement within a few years.

Reeves and I spend a lot of time here. I write out here a lot now, and he plays at his water table, in the sandbox, or on the Swurfer swing we have hanging from the big, live oak tree in the back corner of the fenced-in yard.

"The direct sun isn't on us yet. We can sit if you like. Can I get you a glass of iced tea?" Once the sun starts making its way west, it beams down, but that doesn't begin until around two in the afternoon. I point to an oversized white rocking chair, and he accepts.

"I am fine, thank you. I am still full from lunch. What a great backyard. I didn't remember the cleared area being so big. And the deck makes it. You've made a really nice home here, Hollis. I'm happy for you guys."

"Thank you. We have enjoyed it. Thanks for telling me about it that night and renting it to me. You have no idea how much I needed that direction."

There is an awkward silence with the mention of *that* night. I guess leaving it unsaid has allowed us to both act like that never happened. Now, there is no avoiding it.

TWENTY-SEVEN

Grayson
———————

2:01 pm EST

I THINK Mr. Bojangles would fetch this tennis ball until the sun goes down if I keep throwing it for him. I swear we have been doing this for the better part of an hour while Hollis and I have been talking. My left arm hasn't gotten this much action since I was on the rowing team in college.

Throwing the tennis ball has helped keep my eyes off Hollis's chest. She is wearing a loose, linen shirt with a few buttons near the top. And they are all three undone. I immediately noticed her bronze, smooth skin at the beach, and my eyes kept returning there.

I've been waiting for a husband or partner to show up or come up. She has made it a point to only refer to herself and Reeves. There is no ring in sight and no tan line. I'm guessing she wouldn't have invited me to her house if there was a man in her life. Not that she was doing anything more than showing me the house, which I own. But, still.

167

I wish it were obvious. Or there was a way for me to ask without asking. The wonder is killing me.

I sit down, exhausted from my last throw. I think Mr. Bojangles is finally spent, too, as he didn't come back up the three steps to bring me the ball, falling to lay in the shaded grass instead.

"Well, I better get out of your hair. I've hijacked enough of your day." She is right. Two o'clock on the dot, and that sun is cooking. I've got a call at three anyway.

"I've enjoyed it. It's been really nice to catch up. Thanks for coming by."

"I'll be here for two weeks, so maybe we will run into each other again."

"Well, I have a lot of time on my hands since it is just me with Reeves gone. I'm sure I'll be out on the town like no other." She laughs as she says this. That is the sexy laugh I remember from that night. It still does it to me.

Okay, she is totally telling me there is no one else. Right? Hopeful thinking? "Now that I know you like Sacred Grounds, too, maybe we could grab a cup of coffee or something?"

Did I really tell her we should meet for coffee? I have really regressed. I want a reason to see her again, so throwing out coffee seems like the least scary suggestion in the event there is someone else. What I want to do is invite her over for a slumber party again so I can have a do-over.

"That would be nice. I never turn down a coffee invite."

"Fantastic. I'll reach out, and we can find a time that works for you." I am guessing she has the same number. But if she doesn't, I can get it from Everly. "I don't have much going on, but I do have to go out of town for a ribbon-cutting, and I need to make sure I don't have any more obligations with that before I say for sure when."

"Sounds good. And if your schedule fills up, no worries. If it works, it works. Like I said, I have an open calendar."

She is very laissez faire. That quiet confidence I was so drawn to that night is still there. I like it. There is no hint of desperation there, which is a complete turn-on.

"Here, we can go out of the side gate since you're walking."

I follow her down the steps and across the thick St. Augustine grass. She unhooks the black metal latch, and the gate swings out.

As I take that first step through the gate, several sensations and conflicting thoughts course through me. Physically, it's as though an invisible weight lifts from my shoulders but simultaneously settles in the pit of my stomach, a peculiar contradiction.

My body feels lighter, almost as if an intangible burden has been lifted, yet there's a lingering sense of something left unsaid, a puzzle unfinished. The air around me feels charged, the now hot and sunny day brightening the landscape around me. I don't know what to say awkwardly, so I keep walking, raising my hand in a sort of backward wave, never turning back around. If I do, I might not leave. "I'll be in touch."

Once again, I walk away from her. Only this time, I am determined not to let this be goodbye.

TWENTY-EIGHT

Hollis
_____

4:27 pm EST

> Hey K! Come by my house when you get off. I ran into Grayson earlier at the beach, and then he came by my house to see the changes we had made after the fire. AND he met Reeves. I want to tell you everything and get your insight on how we left things.

I RESISTED GOING to see Kendall at Sacred Grounds. She usually runs around and is busy at the end of her shift.

She gets off at 4:30, so hopefully, she can come by. She is still working at the coffee shop part-time, but her primary source of income is managing social media for beauty products and influencers.

Who knew you could make such a great living off of that? She stays working at Sacred Grounds not for the money but because she says it is part of her identity. She loves the connections she has with most of the regulars that come in there.

I know her dream is to open her own coffee shop. That is where her soul is. I so hope for that for her.

It vibrates as soon as I put my phone down on the table and resume my position with my hands on my keyboard. I glance down and expect to see a response from Kendall. Instead, it's a text from Grayson.

> Hi Hollis. Wondering if you're up for dinner tonight? Last minute, so I understand if you've already got something going on. You mentioned today you had never been to Cafe Pamlico. They have a table if you're available to join me.

It's a simple message asking if I want to join him for dinner. The words seem straightforward, but the implications are anything but. My heart rate speeds up, and a swarm of incongruous emotions ping pong through me.

This raises questions I'm not quite ready to answer. And dilemmas I am not prepared to face. Is this a friendly dinner, a nice effort by him to get me into a restaurant I have been wanting to try for years? Or does it hold a deeper meaning?

My feelings are in disarray. On one hand, I've spent years building a life for Reeves and me, finding my footing as a mother and creating a sense of stability I had longed for. I've finally found solid ground beneath my feet, and this invitation feels like a ripple in the calm waters of my life. Do I want to risk ruffling that?

Yet, on the other hand, the curiosity about Grayson, the connection we shared, and the sense of unfinished business - all gnaw at the edges of my resolve. It's a mix of emotions, to be sure. After our first encounter, I learned never to assume that I know Grayson Sterling's intentions.

Overshadowing it all, though, is the big fat lie that is between us. Can I see him and get to know him more with that albatross? Don't I have to come clean? I don't think I am ready for that. I don't know how I would work through all that, not only with my own heart but dealing with his reaction to the betrayal, and then, most importantly, how to explain it to sweet, innocent Reeves.

What a mess.

My night is wide open, and I feel like letting this opportunity pass me by would be a waste. It could be nothing.

Or, it could be everything.

As I stare at the message, I grapple with the ambiguity of this dinner invitation, as if the words on the screen will reveal more than the letters there.

With a deep breath, I reach for the phone and begin typing a message to Kendall before even thinking about responding to him.

> Okay, I really need you. Grayson just texted and asked if I'd go to dinner with him. I don't know what to do... I need you. If you can't come by when you leave, please call me ASAP!!!!

...

The undulating three dots have me paralyzed. She is responding! I can't do anything until I know what she is typing. Holding the phone, staring, I wait for her message to pop up. Tell me what to do, Kendall. Come on. You always have the right thing to say to me.

> I am getting ready to leave. I can't come by right now, but I say DO IT! What do you have to lose? Plus, isn't your mom picking up Reeves today to stay with them for the week in VA? You deserve a night out. Just don't expect anything to come of it. I'll call you in a little bit.

TWENTY-NINE

Grayson

7:14 pm EST

THE SUN DIPS below the horizon, casting a warm, golden glow on the familiar path to the front door. The street is quiet, only the sound of the rustling treetops breaking the silence. I steal my nerves with a deep breath as we pull in front of her house.

I have been kicking myself for years for just letting her go. I feel like the universe is giving me a second chance. I never got a definitive answer to my internal question of whether she has a partner or a husband. From my informal recon, it appears not, and I figure the best way to find out, without asking, is to ask her out.

Olivier puts the vehicle in park, and the locks automatically disengage. The click is louder than usual. I open the car door. My heart quickens with anticipation. I walk up the path, the gravel crunching beneath my feet. I raise my hand to knock, but the door opens before I get the chance.

There she stands. Hollis is even more beautiful than when I left just a few hours ago. Her eyes meet mine, an unsaid connection between us. My breath catches in my chest, and for a moment, words escape me.

"Hey, there," she says, her voice sweet with a touch of shyness. Her bag is already on her shoulder, and her keys are in hand. Her smile, though cautious, is light and effortless. It's as if the years between us have faded away.

"Hello, you. I am excited for you to experience my favorite restaurant. Are you ready to taste the best food you've had this year?"

"I've been looking forward to this for forever." She smiles and closes the door behind her as we walk together to the car.

I've been looking forward to this for forever, too. I just don't tell her that. I've barely only admitted it to myself.

————

9:29 PM *EST*

DINNER DOES NOT DISAPPOINT. I recommend the swordfish, and it is a winner. There isn't a crumb left on her plate.

Our conversation has been and continues to be easy, just like I remembered it.

I learned about her most recent published novels. She said she was in Los Angeles not too long ago, and I felt a pang of regret that I didn't know. If I had, I would have certainly gone to the reading. My mind flashes back to the dream I had years ago. I still think about it periodically. All of it was so real.

I make a mental note to order some of her books for an insight into how she thinks and the things she writes about. Mystery is her primary genre, and the idea of her solving puzzles in her mind excites me.

It is evident from how she talks that no man is in her life. She said she has only talked to her ex-husband a few times since they divorced. The last time was years ago. He must be Reeves's father, but he doesn't appear to be in his life.

We talk briefly about Reeves. I ask a few questions about what he likes to do, but the conversation turns to other things, and I don't want to press.

In the past, the distance between us, geographically and in circumstance, led me not to pursue further contact. My work on the West Coast consumed my time and energy, and I assumed that a connection formed on the East Coast would ultimately lead nowhere. But now I am motivated to figure out how to bridge that, to see her more, to continue to get to know her.

In all these years, I've never been able to shake the thought of her, the memory of our passionate night. That has to mean something. There is something more profound with her than with any woman I have ever known.

She has a glow about her. When she talks, everything around us fades. I am captivated by her charm, strength, and her natural beauty. Everything she says is interesting. Through her experiences and life on the Outer Banks with her son, I feel myself living vicariously through her.

As we talk, share stories, and gaze into each other's eyes, I can't help but wonder if there's a chance for us. The longing I've felt for her, despite the years that have passed, erases all doubts and excuses I have made in my mind over the years. I find myself pondering whether I want to try or see if the spark that once ignited between us still has the potential to become something.

My intentions remain veiled to me. I grapple with the uncharted territory of our connection and what the future might hold. For now, I'm content to savor this moment, to rediscover Hollis and see where this unexpected reunion might lead.

"Hollis, there's something I've wanted to say for a long time. I'm sorry for disappearing the way I did after that night. I should have reached out, and I should have been more present."

I want to tell her more. I want to excuse it for the wildfire that was my life at that moment. But that feels shallow, so I don't. No matter what, it was a shit move.

Her gaze meets mine, and I can see a mixture of emotions in her eyes. It's a moment of vulnerability for both of us, and I wait for her response, uncertain of what she might say. Unsure of what she thinks, if she even remembers that.

She takes a deep breath, her voice gentle as she replies, "Grayson, it's in the past now. We were both in different places, and I understand that. It's been a long time. Don't think another minute about it. I appreciate your apology, but please don't worry."

Her words have a sense of closure, and I'm grateful for her understanding. It's a small step toward addressing the unspoken questions that have lingered between us for years, and it's a conversation I've longed to have.

But something in her voice gives me a nagging feeling there is something she isn't saying.

THIRTY

Hollis
———————

10:39 pm EST

WITH MY TEA IN HAND, Mr. Bojangles and I walk out to the back deck, the cool evening breeze cooling the warm day. It is strange being home almost a full day now without Reeves. We had our morning on the beach to start the day, but that seems like a lifetime ago now.

I smile to myself as I reflect on the unexpected evening that has unfolded with Grayson. The events of the night swirl in my mind. It was a good night. I enjoyed being with him, much to my dismay.

I now realize I prefer thinking of him as this untouchable, grumpy, off-limits guy. But he was totally down to earth, charming and interesting. I am feeling those same yearnings for him that started bubbling up that night at his beach house.

I take a deep breath and decide to call Kendall to share the details of the dinner. She called me before I left with Grayson and encouraged me to let down my guard and see where the night took us. I took her advice, and now I worry that my heart is vulnerable again.

"Hey, Kendall," I say as she answers. "I need to tell you about tonight. You have some time to talk?"

Her voice on the other end of the line is warm and reassuring. "Of course. In fact, I am just heading home and about two minutes from your house. How about I stop by?"

"Sure, just come out back. I am sitting on the deck. Hurry!"

The crickets and bullfrogs are having a concert, the beat in perfect harmony. The sounds of summer nights at the beach haven't changed my whole life. Some may find this noisy, but to me, it is one of the most beautiful songs by nature, comforting and lulling.

Like clockwork, about three minutes later the back door opens, and out comes my sweet friend. After everything that has happened today, seeing her tonight is exactly what I need to organize all of this in my head. My sounding board.

I jump up and we hug. I offer her something to drink, and we start off talking about her night. She had a third date with a guy she met through a dating site. She isn't into him but is allowing herself some time to see if things progress. The thought of getting on one of those sites sends my brain into a tizzy.

"I say if you aren't feeling it by the third date, he isn't the one. Don't be with him just to be with a man. Trust me on this one. It won't end well."

She knows full well my history. She gets it.

With this, my mind goes to my marriage with Benton. Great guy, but he wasn't my guy, and I was living with mild depression for years. I am much happier being single than staying with a man I was not in love with.

"I know. I am just ready to meet someone. Maybe I am just too damn picky." She takes a deep breath and then exhales deeply. Exasperated.

"Enough about me. Tell me about Grayson! This is so wild y'all ran into each other at the beach and then went to dinner. How was it? Don't leave out a thing!"

"We did kiss when he walked me to the door."

"Wait, what?! Y'all kissed? Why are you just now telling me this? How was it?!"

"Umm, it was freaking amazing. I was melting as his lips touched mine. He might be the best kisser I have ever kissed in my life." Not that I've kissed a lot of men. But I feel confident that he is quite skilled in that department.

I am wet remembering the kiss—the desire to not stop there.

"Did I tell you he has a driver? Anyway, he got out and walked me to the door when we got to my house. He didn't ask to come in or invite me to his house, which I thought was very gentlemanly. Especially since I didn't have the strength to resist before."

"Okay, this is getting better by the second. I'm dying for you!"

"I wanted to invite him in, but I resisted. Everything is just happening so fast and the fact that he doesn't know my son is also his son is right there at the forefront of my mind. I keep thinking that I have to tell him if I keep seeing him."

"Well, yes, eventually. But right now, you can explore this. How many years has it been since you've had sex?! Girl, go for it if you're feeling it. You have this time alone. Just remember what I said--don't expect anything."

"That is why I left it with the one kiss. As hard as that was."

She listens intently as I recount the evening, the conversation with Grayson, and his apology for disappearing after our night together. I can sense Kendall's thoughtful consideration. There's a pause, and then she offers her insight.

"Hollis, it's clear that he came into this with an intention. The apology was a way for him to open up a conversation. But you must remember your boundaries and what's best for you and Reeves."

Her words resonate with me, and I appreciate her perspective. I can't help but feel guarded with Grayson. I remain uncertain about the complexities of our past and the existence of a son he doesn't know about. There is no doubt that minor detail further complicates what this could mean.

Does he intend for me to be his side piece when he is in town? Is there even a way for us to be more than that? And if not, am I okay with that?

Kendall's advice is empathetic and practical, as always. "If you sleep with him, it doesn't mean it has to go anywhere else. I mean, last time you slept with him, you went almost five years without speaking. What's to say that won't happen again? Then you get one night of hot sex, and then you can figure out how or if telling him about Reeves is the right thing to do."

She says this last part with a laugh. Funny, not funny.

She does have a point, though. If we do sleep together, it doesn't mean I have to come clean. Yet.

Or do I? This is so hard. His being completely out of my life made putting that on the back burner much easier.

Her words give me a sense of clarity and a reminder to prioritize my well-being and my son's future. The evening has opened up a world of possibilities, and I must navigate it with care and thoughtfulness.

"It is exciting. Regardless. He is hot as shit! If you can separate your feelings, I say at least go for a passionate, sexy roll in the hay. See if he is as good as you remember."

She pauses, and I take a sip of tea. Would I be okay with just a hookup? It has been a while, and I could use a little attention in that area. And Reeves is out of town, so it can't hurt, right?

"But if you feel yourself falling for him at all, I would say abort. Because you don't want to go down that path. If Reeves weren't part of the equation, taking the risk may not be a big deal. But the stakes are too high. So really think about that."

That is all I have been able to think about. Well, that and feeling like I am lying by not telling him the whole truth.

"It is getting late, so I am going to call it a night. Keep me posted on what happens. Based on today, I would be surprised if you don't hear from him tomorrow. Just let it ride and see where things go."

We hug and I walk her through the house to the front door.

"Be safe driving home. Love you, my sweet friend. I couldn't do life without you!"

She blows a kiss as she gets into her car. I thank God every day for this dear friend. I am fortunate for her companionship and guidance.

As her tail lights disappear down the road, I make the decision to ride my bike to the beach. It is a sudden one, driven by an inexplicable restlessness that's been building in me since this morning at the beach. I no longer get the opportunity for my night rides, so I seize the chance to hop on and get a dose of late-night salt air.

As I start pedaling, the contrasting cool breeze and warm mid-August night envelop me in a gentle embrace. The weather is still warm enough for short sleeves, but it's not hot. The moon casts a soft, silvery glow on the road, lighting the short ride to the beach. It's the kind of night where the world seems to hold its breath, the stillness broken only by the occasional movement of the trees above.

The quiet town feels like my own private sanctuary, a backdrop to my wandering thoughts. The streets are deserted, and the air has eerie tranquility.

I pedal towards the beach, my mind on overdrive. Thoughts of Grayson and the sparks that have been rekindled occupy my every waking moment. I can't shake the memory of our past, and the possibility of a future together lingers like an elusive dream.

The rhythmic hum of my bicycle tires against the quiet night's backdrop begins to lull me into a contemplative trance.

As I approach the bend in the road, my heart quickens with a sudden realization. The beam of headlights pierces the darkness, blinding me momentarily. Panic surges through my veins as I instinctively swerve to the side, my heart racing with fear.

And then, everything goes black.

THIRTY-ONE

Grayson

11:17 pm EST

MY INSIDES ARE INVERTED, my stomach in my throat as I process the gravity of the situation. Olivier hit a fucking bicyclist. Jesus Christ.

Not to mention, this person could have been seriously injured. He was driving me while on the clock when he did it. I take a deep breath, steadying myself.

I asked him to pick me up after a long walk on the beach after dinner. Once I realized I was further away from home than I wanted to be and that I was close to the Sanderling, where Olivier was staying, I called and asked if he would pick me up and drive me back to the house.

Why the fuck didn't I just turn around and walk my lazy ass back? This is a nightmare.

I jump out of the car to see if the person is okay. "Please, God, let this person be okay," I say out loud, sincerely hoping it is just a minor bump. We couldn't have been going any more than fifteen miles an hour.

I realize it is a female and that she isn't moving. Olivier bends down to check her. "Is she all right, Olivier?" I ask, a sense of urgency creeping into my voice.

"She seems to be okay," he reassures me, though there's an underlying unease in his tone. "Ma'am, are you okay?"

I walk up. If he is talking to her, she must be conscious. As soon as I look down, I see that it's Hollis lying there, her bike mangled about ten feet away on the ground. My heart shatters, and the air is knocked out of my lungs.

"Hollis. Oh, my God. I am so sorry. Olivier didn't see you! Are you okay?" I kneel beside her, stroking the hair out of her face. I have an urge to protect her like I've never had in my life for anyone.

She tries to sit up, but Olivier encourages her to stay put until the paramedics arrive. He dials a number on his phone. I stay with her, trying to reassure her.

I'm thankful that she is awake and there are no visible injuries.

"What hurts?" I ask her as if I can do anything about it more than what we are already doing.

"I can't really tell. Nothing specifically. I just feel a little out of it. I came around the curve and didn't realize you were there until your lights were on me. That is the last thing I remember."

"Well, stay calm. Someone should be here soon."

Red flashing lights approach. They got here quickly, thank goodness.

A wave of anxiety washes over me. I stand up, feeling like I am intruding as the paramedics ask her questions. I don't want to leave her, but I want to give her privacy.

I feel a sense of restlessness. Once again, I am helpless in a situation I feel partly responsible for with regard to Hollis. I pace around, waiting for a word from them.

She is now sitting up on the curb, drinking water. I want to walk over there, but I also want to give her space. I worry she is going to blame me and hate me for this.

Finally, one of the young men, Jason, who has been with her since arriving, comes over to update Olivier and me.

"She is a little banged up but doesn't appear to have any broken bones. Because she lost consciousness for a moment, we want to take her in to be examined for a concussion. She says she is fine and has refused to ride in with us. She wants you to drive her."

His words comfort me. She must still trust me.

"We will definitely take her. Thank you for letting us know what is going on. Anything in particular we should relay at the hospital?"

"Just let them know she was involved in a pedestrian-vehicle accident and that she lost consciousness for a moment upon impact. She may have to stay the night to be observed."

The paramedics notified the local police department of the accident, per protocol. Two cruisers pull up, and I walk up to them immediately to introduce myself and let them know what is happening. I recognize Officer Creedmore from our run-in a few years ago. Everything comes full circle.

After she gets my side of the story, she walks over to speak with Hollis. I find myself engrossed in watching Hollis as they talk. She is still sitting and looking up, her smile evident even from this far.

Hollis says she is not pressing charges because it was a freak accident. It was determined that Olivier wasn't speeding. Because of the hill and the curve, they didn't see each other until the last moment, when it was too late to avoid the crash.

The other officer, whose name I didn't catch, writes an incident report, and Olivier and Hollis sign it. If something does end up coming out about this, there will be a report detailing what happened. To say I am relieved is an understatement. Now, to get her better.

How quickly life can take unexpected turns.

"Hollis, Olivier, and I will drive you to the hospital to be checked out. Is that okay with you?"

"You don't have to do that. They said I am fine. I just want to go home and sleep it off. I will let you give me a ride to the house if you don't mind. My bike might be done for."

"It's crucial they take a look just to be sure. I will stay with you if that is okay with you. Please let me take you."

"Okay, you are quite convincing." Her smile arrests me. "I will go on the one condition that you buy me a new bike." We both laugh. I am relieved that she seems to be back to her easy demeanor.

"Deal. We can go pick one out when you're feeling up to it! But for now, let's get you to the Outer Banks Hospital." With that, I reach my arm down to assist her off the curb.

She stands up and takes a moment to make sure she has her footing.

I walk her to the Range Rover and help her in, closing the door behind her. Something about her allowing me to help her, even in an insignificant way, empowers me. Like I am finally doing something for her. I want to be a part of the solution, not the problem.

THIRTY-TWO

Hollis

———

Outer Banks Hospital

Nags Head, NC

Sunday, August 13th

12:03 *am EST*

AS WE AWAIT the doctor's return, Grayson puts a second pillow behind me. He is so attentive, and the concern in his eyes is totally endearing. I suddenly feel like a love-sick teenager. Maybe it was the knock on my head.

I catch a glimpse of his perfect lips as he leans down to fluff my pillows. I harken back to the kiss at my door after dinner. And my wish for more.

I lean up and kiss him. He looks surprised at first, completely caught off guard. And then he cradles my head in his hand and supports me as we both give in to what is unmistakably between us. There is no holding back.

Just as I lose myself in him, a man clears his throat beside my bed. Grayson pulls back, and I begrudgingly turn my head to see a man in his mid-forties standing beside me with a white lab coat and a clipboard.

"Pardon me. I just wanted to introduce myself. I am Doctor Jones. I am the attending on call tonight. How are you feeling?"

Well, that was awkward.

———

1:55 *am EST*

THE HOSPITAL ROOM is bathed in a sterile, fluorescent glow, its clinical aura starkly contrasting the thoughts swirling through my head. I wish Grayson would have just let me go home. I let him convince me because I genuinely value that he cared enough to push me on the point.

It's almost two in the morning. I'm propped up in a hospital bed, the white linens crisp and unforgiving. Grayson is dozing in the green pleather chair in the corner. He is a good man to be here so late. I am feeling terrible we are still here. This could take all night.

Gingerly, I touch my smarting arm, wincing a little. The myriad of bruises and aches are primarily on my right hip and left elbow. Nothing is broken, Doctor Jones has confirmed, but the pain reminds me that this shit is real, and it could have been much worse. I am waiting for the results of the MRI of my brain.

I wish I could rest my eyes, too. But my brain won't be quiet. It is like the universe is screaming at us today, pushing us together now four times in less than twenty-four hours. If my body didn't ache so, I'd swear someone was punking me.

And that kiss. It injected me with an energy that is still bouncing throughout my body like a live wire.

A nurse walks in, her eye on the machine hooked up to me, monitoring my vitals. Grayson awakens with a start, sitting up quickly. He looks shocked. "How could I have fallen asleep," I hear him grumble aloud.

"Everything looks good, the nurse tells me. The MRI shows that you have no internal bleeding in your skull. You may have a slight concussion, so you should have someone stay with you tonight to keep an eye on you. Otherwise, you're free to go."

Once again, I'll call Kendall in the middle of the night to ask her to babysit me. I'll have Olivier drop me off there instead of home.

Once the nurse steps out, I pull out my phone to text Kendall.

Before I can do that, Grayson pipes up. "I know you're going to think I am trying to get fresh," he says. "But I promise my intentions are pure. Can I play nurse for you tonight? I promise to behave. I want to be able to check on you periodically. Honestly, it is the least I can do."

At this moment, feeling uncharacteristically frisky, I wouldn't mind too much if his intentions were a little naughty. Where is this coming from?!

"Oh, Grayson, you've done more than enough. I will call Kendall, a friend who lives up the street from me. If you can give me a ride there, she can make sure I don't kick the bucket in the night. But thank you for the offer."

"It is two in the morning. Unless she is already up partying or something, just let me do this for you. My driver almost ran you over, after all. It is the least you can do. Well, that and buy you a new bike."

His concern is incredibly endearing. He is right. It is very late. Maybe I will take him up on the offer instead of trying to fight him on this.

And maybe we can play nurse and patient after all.

"Plus, the sheets were just changed this morning. You can have the bedroom you stayed in before. I'll make sure you're set-up, and then you can rest in a familiar setting."

I want to remind him that I am only somewhat familiar with two rooms in his house. But we aren't there yet. It's too soon to joke about that night.

"No, I will have to draw the line there. I will stay at your house on the condition that you allow me to sleep in a guest room."

"Okay, I will concede to that if you agree to stay. It's settled, then. Let's go. You need to get some rest so that we can get you healed. Is there anything you need from your house before we go to mine?"

"Deal. I hate to ask, but do you mind if Mr. Bojangles stays with me? I hate to leave him by himself."

"Of course! We will stop by on the way and grab him. Thank you for letting me do this for you, Hollis."

THIRTY-THREE

Grayson
_____

3 N Baum Trail

Duck, NC 27949

Monday, August 14th

8:12 *am EST*

MY PHONE BUZZES on the bedside table. It is a text from Olivier.

> I left the groceries on the front doorstep for you. The milk and eggs will need to be refrigerated soon. I didn't want them staying out too long. The sun will be bearing down before you know it. Enjoy!

I swear, Olivier is my secret weapon in my quest to slay life. I texted him in the middle of the night as I drifted off to sleep. It occurred to me that I had to make Hollis breakfast.

I asked him to go shopping for me. Three in the morning is a little too late to line someone to come cook this morning for breakfast. So, I will be breaking out my Gordon Ramsay skills to whip something up.

I sent him a list of what I could think of but asked him to fill in with anything he saw that would be a good addition to my breakfast plans. I hope there is something in there that I can manage without killing her in the process.

I remember the burnt toast that morning and smile to myself. I was wound up so tightly and annoyed, and she was so cute and flustered, so eager to please. God, I'm an ass.

I head out to get the bags. When I come downstairs, Mr. Bojangles greets me.

"What are you doing out here, Old Man? Do you need to go out?"

His tail is wagging, and his eyes are twinkling at me. I notice grey on his face that wasn't there before. It highlights how much time is between us.

He is a great dog. I can't believe I ever thought he would attack me that first day. He is the furthest thing from an attack dog. I can't imagine a more docile, loving animal. I think most cats would do more damage than he would.

I walk him to the door with me, holding him back with my left on his collar as I make sure there is a path clear of grocery bags for him to get by. As soon as I let go, he bounds down the steps and is at the bottom before I can even straighten up. I run after him, nervous he might run off. I can't take another calamity involving Hollis, especially not now that she's officially on my watch.

He is squatting in the front yard, and it doesn't appear he will break free. I realize I don't have a leash, so I hope he follows me back after relieving himself. I am near enough that if he does make a run for it, I can grab him.

He stands up and looks at me like, "What is your problem?"

I laugh and ask him, "Want to cook for your mom? I have lots of food."

With the word food, his ears perk up. He makes a dash for the steps and heads up. I wish I could still take steps three at a time like that. I have no idea if Hollis brought any food for him, but I can find something in there for him to eat.

———

9:02 *am EST*

I PULL out the rattan trays my mom brought to the beach house one Fourth of July week when my entire family came out here for vacation.

I was in and out with work the whole time, but everyone got to enjoy the house and the beach that week. It might have been the last time we were all together.

I placed a plate of scrambled eggs, sausage, and strawberries on the tray first. Then, a small bowl of oatmeal and a small plate holding a slice of toast with a pat of butter and a spoonful of grape jam. I put a glass of orange juice in the right corner, fold a napkin, and place a fork on it. I look it over, making sure I haven't forgotten anything.

"Water," I say out loud. "She needs some water and some ibuprofen." I grab a big crystal glass from the cabinet and fill it with filtered water. I run upstairs, grab a bottle of ibuprofen, and bring it down, getting four out. I place them in a small ramekin. Okay, I think this covers it.

I pick up the tray and walk carefully down the hall to the guest room, being careful not to slosh the OJ or water. I hate to wake her, but part of the reason she needed to be with someone is to make sure she is okay.

The door is cracked, about half-open. There seems to be just enough room for Mr. Bojangles to slip out, which is probably why it is ajar.

I peek through and see her sleeping peacefully in the bed, the covers pulled up. I want to sit here and watch her, appreciating her long lashes resting on her cheeks. But I feel a little creepy.

I gently push the door open and walk in. I set the tray quietly on the end of the bed and go to the closet to get the luggage stand. I set it up beside her and put the tray on top.

When I pick up the tray, she stirs and then opens one eye to spot me. "Good morning, you. How are you feeling?" A lump immediately surfaces in my throat, and it turns out she isn't the only one waking up right now.

"I feel like I got hit by a truck. How about you?"

"Very funny. Because you did. I feel like the jerk who is responsible." I sit beside her on the edge of the bed. "How is that elbow?"

She pulls it out of the covers and bends it a few times. "It is a little tight, but it is okay." There is a bandage on it, protecting the asphalt burn she received when she must have landed on it. It is the only outward sign she had an accident last night. The goose egg in her hairline isn't visible.

"I made you some breakfast. I am no fine chef, but I knew you would need something to eat. And if I am being honest, I wanted a reason to come see you. I also brought you some ibuprofen if you need some for the pain."

"I feel surprisingly okay. I guess we will see once I get up. But I am starving, so thank you. Have you eaten?"

"I snacked while I cooked. Oh, and Mr. Bojangles has eaten, too. He said he liked Cheerios, so that is what I gave him. He gobbled it up like he hadn't eaten in days. Are you neglecting him?!"

She laughs at this. "I brought him food when I packed a bag last night. I'm sure he would much more prefer Cheerios to what I brought for him. Thank you for doing that."

I clear my throat. I haven't ever had a dog, so how was I to know he shouldn't have Cheerios?

"He already went out, but I think I will take him for a walk and get you a coffee at Sacred Grounds. Did you bring a leash, too?"

She nods and turns back the covers as if about to get up.

"You don't have to get it. Just tell me where to find it. What is your drink of choice there?"

"Look at you, Mr. Perfect! The leash is hanging on the back of the door there," she says, pointing to the sliding door out to the deck. "And if you're going, I would love a large latte with oat milk, please. This breakfast looks fabulous, thank you. You're doing too much! Thank you!"

"It is truly my pleasure." I lean down and kiss her on the forehead, wishing for more but more than willing to settle for any touch. I stand up and open the armoire, revealing a large flat-screen television. I grab the remote from the shelf and put it on the bed beside her.

"Please help yourself to whatever you need. I should be back in about thirty minutes."

THIRTY-FOUR

Hollis

9:39 am EST

I AM BLOWN AWAY. Who is this man? He caters to my every need and cares for my dog while he does it! Is he trying to make me fall in love with him? Because he is doing a damn good job if so.

My mind is swimming with thoughts, and all I want to do is find my phone to call Kendall and give her an update. And get her take on it all.

My mind immediately goes to Reeves. First, I need to check in with them. I pull out my phone and call my mom to see what amazingness they are up to today.

I was able to talk to him before he went to bed last night before dinner, but he has been up for three hours by now. They are on the run doing something active and fantastic, no doubt.

And then I am reminded of the dark secret I am harboring. I have to tell Grayson. I can't keep seeing him like this, letting him care for me like this, knowing I am keeping this huge, significant thing from him.

But first, I need to pee. I hear the front door close once they leave, giving me the all-clear to get out of bed. I pull the covers aside and walk to the bathroom. I'm limping a little. Not so much from soreness but because everything is stiff.

The familiarity of this room surrounds me, offering a sanctuary of sorts. It looks exactly as I remember it from all of those years ago. That morning, it was all a shade of gray. But after he left, I came into the room and sat on the bed, thinking about that night, wondering if I would ever come in here again or see him. And now look where we are.

I didn't know I was pregnant with his child at that time. I hadn't rented the house down the street, although I knew I wanted it even then before seeing it. There was no fire. I hadn't met Kendall. So much has changed in my world since then, but this room has stayed the same.

I fish my phone out of my bag along with a charger, and I get back in bed, eager to talk to Reeves. It rings and rings, and finally, my mom's voicemail comes on. Knowing Crazy Roberta, they have been at the farmer's market since it opened.

I hang up and call Kendall. She answers on the first ring.

"So, did you end up seeing him last night…?"

Her voice is cheerful and flirty. She must think that with an early morning call, I have some news for her since we parted ways only a few hours ago.

"Well, as it turns out, I did…"

I give her all the juice, including the kiss at the hospital. She is beside herself, living vicariously through me, so she says.

I am sufficiently stuffed. I don't usually eat this much for breakfast, so my body is extra full. I take a big sip of the orange juice. It is tangy and cold on my tongue. It is so refreshing I could drink the whole glass if it didn't feel like I have food stacked up to my esophagus. He must think I am a ravenous, crazy person bringing me all this.

I grab two ibuprofen for good measure and pop them in my mouth, followed by a swig of water.

I get up, put the tray back on the stand beside the bed, and stretch. I can feel some soreness everywhere. I bend down to touch my feet, stretching my lower back. Really, the worst ache is my elbow. And that is from the scrape. Incredibly, I can black out for a second, and a scraped elbow is the worst injury to show for it.

I hear the front door open and the familiar taps on the hard floor as I hear Mr. Bojangles barreling down the hall. He comes directly into the bedroom, followed by the most handsome man holding two paper cups and a big smile on his face.

Mr. Bojangles jumps up on me, almost pushing me back on the bed. It is nice to feel so loved. I bend down, kiss him on the head, and look up at Grayson, our eyes meeting.

"The breakfast was amazing. I couldn't finish it all, but it was perfect. You're doing too much. Thank you. How was the big guy on the walk? Did he pull you too much?"

"He was great. He's a celebrity there, so being his wingman this morning was fun. Several people asked about you. But I didn't know how much you would want to disclose, so I didn't mention the accident. I just said I wanted the privilege of walking this love magnet."

I beam with pride. He is very loved by everyone who meets him. Hearing Grayson go on and on about him is so endearing. Even after Mr. Bojangles backed him into the bathroom. Everyone is redeemable to some degree.

"It would have been fine, but that is okay, too. Saved you from having to go into it."

"How are you feeling? Up for sitting on the deck to watch the morning unfold on the beach?" As he says this, he reaches his hand out to me with what I assume is my coffee. I reach out to take it, and our hands brush each other and linger for a moment longer than necessary. The blood rushes through me, causing me to take a deep breath.

"I feel great, thank you. And I would love that. It's my favorite morning wake-up ritual." There is one other morning ritual I might like better. I surprise myself for letting my mind go there and try to shake it off as I follow him to the sliding door leading to the deck.

Like Pavlov's dog, I can't help letting my eyes land on his tight rear end, watching it as he walks ahead of me.

THIRTY-FIVE

Grayson
———————

10:18 am

"YOU KNOW you really scared me last night," I tell Hollis. "When I realized it was you, I almost lost it. I've never felt that worried about another human in my life."

"Wow. You were that concerned about little 'ol me? Thank you for all you did and are doing to take care of me. Makes a girl feel special."

"Hollis, I want you to know that I haven't stopped thinking about you since that night we shared. Here on this deck. Every time I have been in this town since then, I wonder where you are and what you are doing. I know this is a lot. Please forgive me. Something about a near-death experience that gets me all mushy."

I pause for a minute, gathering my thoughts. I surprise even myself blurting that out. I hadn't planned to say it, but sitting here with her in this place, imagining what would have happened if the accident had been worse, it is spilling out of me. I feel like I can't miss the opportunity again.

"I don't know what it is about you," I continue. "When we met, I had a lot of things going on both with work and personally. And I was an ass that next morning. But the time we spent together, while it was short, has been with me since. I have never felt the way I did when I was with you."

She is watching me intently but not saying a word. I can't read what it means. My heart is beating fast and hard. This whole new lease on life has me not even recognizing myself. I have never put myself out there like this with a woman. And now I know why.

"Say anything. Even if it is that you think I am crazy. Because I totally am."

"I don't think you're crazy at all. I honestly don't know what to say." She pauses, and I feel deflated. The moment is heavy with silence.

She continues, "I can tell you that I haven't stopped thinking about you, either. I figured with how things ended that morning that you didn't feel the same way, so I tried to put it and you out of my mind."

A glimmer of hope. I feel giddy at the notion that she thought of me afterward.

"I apologize for that. Right after I woke up that morning, I found out some very unfortunate details about the employee who was fraudulently renting out my house, so my head wasn't on straight. Not to mention, I worked really late the night before we met. None of this is an excuse, but trying to give you some insight into the shit-show that was my life at that time. I was a complete jerk with all of it, and I can't apologize enough."

I pour out my heart. I have nothing to lose at this point, and something unexplainable is nudging me to lay it all on the line. I have no idea what I want or what to expect from this, but if I can at least put it out there, maybe I can have peace from now on instead of always looking back with regret.

"Tell me more about the employee! I always wanted to know how that happened and what went down."

I am grateful for a change in subject. The eight-hundred-pound gorilla has been exposed. Let's sit with these unexpected revelations for now. I can tell she is being cautious with what she says. She has no reason to trust me.

I give her the unabridged version of everything that happened with Claire. How she rented the house, how long she had been doing it, all the way to the false sexual harassment allegations and then her plea, including dropping her allegations, and Claire being sentenced to four years in prison.

Of course, she had lots of questions about Claire. I have become so numb to it all after dealing with it for so long that I forgot how fucking insane that whole situation was.

I am glad I haven't heard her name in well over two years. Talking about it again, especially linking it to the time we met, brings all of it back to me. Luckily, it no longer has a negative effect on me. It is just a nutty story of a batshit crazy employee.

I reach over and touch her hand with my index finger. I don't know what possessed me to do that, but I wanted to connect with her physically. She looks down at my hand and then up to meet my eyes. Our gaze is locked on each other, and we remain there momentarily. It is all I can do not to lean in to kiss her.

———

12:32 PM *EST*

I HAPPEN to catch a glimpse of my watch and realize it is after noon. We have been sitting here talking for over two hours. I can't remember the last time I sat and talked to anyone casually for that amount of time and wasn't chomping at the bit to do a hundred other things.

She still has me. Maybe even more now than before. I am completely and wholly captivated by this woman.

We talked a little about her ex-husband. It blows me away that this man squandered his opportunity with this enigma. Not only is she stunningly beautiful, but she is also intelligent and interesting. And funny!

"You must be ready for some lunch. Would you like to walk down to one of your favorite spots for lunch? Are you up for a walk?"

She turns gently, and her profile makes my heart skip a bit. Her smooth, gentle curls are pulled back in a messy bun, highlighting the perfect shape of her head and face. A few naughty strands of hair fall around her face perfectly, blowing in the wind ever so slightly.

"Surprisingly, I am hungry. After that giant breakfast this morning, I didn't think I would ever eat again. I was so full. But I guess my concussion demands lots of food. I would love to walk up to the boardwalk and have lunch if you have time. I feel like I am taking up your whole life these last two days."

The idea of her taking up my life excites me.

"Remember, these two weeks, with a few exceptions, I am completely checked out. I thought I would be alone, so I welcome your company. "

"Same for me! Normally, I would be completely tied to Reeves's schedule, but with him gone, I am atypically free, as well. Let's do it. But speaking of Reeves, do you mind if I call my mom before we leave? I haven't spoken to them yet today."

"Of course not. Please, by all means."

"I will before we leave. I want to freshen up a bit first."

I stand up and crack my back. The day is perfect. Warm, slightly overcast, shielding us from the hot sun, but still bright. Hollis uncrosses her long legs in what feels like slow motion. I want to run my hands up them, feel her again.

She heads toward the guest room. I start toward the living room, but I follow her instead. The heavy door slides easily, and we both step in. I don't move aside when she reaches back to close it behind her. Her body brushes against mine, and the electricity between us is sizzling.

I pull her to me and kiss her passionately. I don't know if she will let me, but I can't resist trying. She wraps her arms around my waist and pulls her body tight to me, her eyes never leaving mine. I can feel her hips pressing into me, telling me that I am welcome.

The space between our faces shrinks until our lips are nearly touching. And then, the world blurs into insignificance. As our mouths meet, her breath entering my mouth, I let go of any self-control I might have left.

Her lips are soft and welcoming, contrasting our messy and bumpy past that had kept us apart for years.

The kiss is gentle, a tentative exploration of what could be. It's not a passionate embrace but rather a communion of our souls. Acknowledging that our long history is inversely proportional to how well we know each other. Yet we are connected and drawn to one another.

My heart races as I pull back slightly, gazing into Hollis's eyes, searching for signs of what this means to her. I don't sense any reluctance on her part. Her body is leaning into me, and she looks up at me, beckoning me back to her lips.

As we pull away from another passionate kiss, I feel a rush of emotions coursing through me, but above all, there's a sense of duty to her. I'm determined to do things differently this time, to forge a new path with Hollis, and to navigate the complexities of our shared history.

THIRTY-SIX

Hollis

12:56 pm EST

WE LINGER on the threshold for several minutes, locked in an epic kiss I would never want to end. Finally, I am feeling his touch again, the touch that I imagined on countless nights and have longed for so long. The subtle but intentional press of our bodies into each other, the memories and questions all leading up to this.

It's clear to me now that our shared story is far from over. The past, present, and future have merged in a way I couldn't have foreseen just two days ago. The uncertainty of what lies ahead fills me, but I focus on the present. And right now, I can't get enough of Grayson Sterling.

The foreplay started yesterday on the beach when we unexpectedly ran into each other. The three of us, an invisible thread connecting us all. And it climaxed on the same deck that was the start years ago. A salty gust of wind rushes through the still-open door, tickling my skin as his strong hands hold me.

As our lips part, a whirlwind of emotions swirls within me. I can't help but pull away, my breath staggering with a mixture of desire and apprehension. The desire wins, hands down.

Grayson pulls his head back, still holding mine with his large, strong hands. His eyes are closed, his lips are full. His handsome features are illuminated by the soft, overcast light reflecting off the ocean. The breeze tousles his thick hair. I have an unbridled, solitary view of this masterpiece of a man.

His eyes are open, bright blue, deep, and fixed on mine. The tension in the air is palpable, a magnetic pull that keeps our bodies tightly together, even now that the kiss is done.

In this moment, I can still taste the sweet connection between us, and I yearn for more of him. All of him. His formidable build, broad shoulders, and square jaw accentuating his rugged handsomeness give me a sense of safety. Something I have never been able to rely on anyone else for.

It is strange because our time together is not much in the grand scheme of things, but our story spans years. I feel like I know him more deeply than anyone I have ever known before. But I also feel the one thing that keeps us tethered is also a wedge between us, not allowing us to fully be close. Until I am completely honest with him, this can never be given a proper chance.

The connection between us is undeniable, but the weight of the past and the secrets I hold weigh heavily on my heart.

The taste of his kiss lingers on my lips, a sweet and tantalizing reminder of our shared history.

My stare is fixed on Grayson, and my eyes beg him to take me. I feel my tender and vulnerable heart opening to him.

I remember how hurt I was the last time I let my heart get too involved, and now I have my son, Reeves, to consider. I can handle a broken heart. I don't think I can handle letting his heart get broken.

It's not just about me anymore.

I can't ruin this moment. I want him more than I have ever wanted anyone. Honesty will have to wait again. Now, raw, primal needs take precedence.

He picks me up and carries me to the bed, still unmade from the night before. The white cotton comforter is rumbled to the side, the top sheet pulled back. It is almost as if it is set for just this exact moment for the two of us to slide in together. I don't have it in me to protest.

He pulls off my thin shorts, revealing that I have nothing on underneath. He bends down and kisses my thigh, sending me into complete surrender to him. His tongue traces from my inner thigh, down my leg, and ends at my foot.

He takes my foot in his hands and rubs it, his big blue eyes coyly looking up at me. I've had a foot massage before, but nothing has ever felt as sensual as this does now.

My body is doing somersaults on the inside, unsure how to process all the physical and mental stimulation that it is receiving.

He unfastens his pants and removes them and his boxer briefs, showcasing his beautiful manhood. I lift my tank top over my head and lie back on the bed. I want Grayson Sterling to devour me. To claim me as his own.

"Take me," I say breathlessly, almost unable to utter the words.

He tosses his own shirt to the side and climbs on top of me.

"Do you have a condom?" I ask hesitantly, not wanting to break the cadence and momentum. But I also know now that I am fertile, and we must be cautious.

He doesn't answer. Instead, he kisses down my chest and between my breasts and then gets up. He picks up his pants off of the floor and removes his wallet, taking out a condom. He slips it on and is back on top of me, assuaging any concerns I had about killing the vibe.

He slides into me, his giant cock filling me. I am wet and ready for him. We fit together perfectly, connecting spiritually and physically. A perfect union.

He is soft and slow at first as I pull my own legs up, making myself more available for him.

"I want you," I whisper in his ear. "I've wanted you for so long."

With these words, he thrusts harder, yelling out as he does. My body shudders as I orgasm. I am almost unable to take any more. The pleasure is more than I can bear. I yell out his name, "Grayson! Grayson, yes! Yes! YES!"

"Hollis. You are perfect. I can't hold back anymore. I am going to come. I. Can't. Ahhh." With that, he falls onto me, his shaft still inside of me. "I'm sorry I couldn't stop it. You're too perfect."

I whisper back to him, "It's okay. I couldn't hold back, either. That is the most intense orgasm I have ever had. And I thought that the first time we made love. You're a God. Thank you."

Did I really thank him for sex? I had no idea how much I needed that. Mind-blowing. That is all I can think of to describe it. All of it. From this morning to the deck, to the freaking kiss of the century. The man deserves a flipping thank you.

We both lay there, our limbs tangled, our skin sticky from the exertion of it all. He pulls himself out of me and falls to the sheets. We are both still breathing heavily, our bodies still coming down from it. I close my eyes and bask in the love.

"May I taste you?" he asks. I am so startled by it. I don't even know how to respond. I am generally not a fan of oral sex, but I can't resist anything from this man. The breeze is still coming in from the open door, and the room is bright. There is no hiding anything like I can in the dark. He can see all of me.

"Yes, please," I respond, my body overriding my brain's usual modesty. "I would love nothing more."

He makes his way down, kissing my stomach as his face descends down my body. As his tongue enters me, my back arches and there is no describing the sounds that came out of me.

THIRTY-SEVEN

Grayson

_____

2:17 pm EST

WE BOTH MUST HAVE DOZED off. When I awake, the room is warm and stagnant. The afternoon sun is coming in hot. With the door open, letting any air conditioning out, the air is thick. Even with just the thin sheet on us, I still need to get my leg out in order to cool off. I am surprised when I look at my watch and realize it's past two in the afternoon.

I am lying on my left side facing Hollis. She is still asleep, her face in perfect stillness. Feeling her skin against mine is even better than I imagined it would have been. The kiss last night after dinner was electric. But that one today… There are no words to describe the feelings that ran up and down my body. To sound cheesy and corny, it was cosmic.

Feeling her soft lips… Just the thought of it stirs a whirlwind of emotions within me. An undeniable bond exists between us, one that has stood the test of time. That kiss today felt like a confirmation on both of our parts that our connection was never really dormant.

As our lips met, I was filled with confidence and a certainty that I want to do things differently this time. The past has taught me the importance of honesty, communication, and respect, and I'm determined to navigate this gift of a possible second chance with a new sense of understanding.

I am acutely aware of Hollis's apprehension. Given our previous encounters, she has every reason to be cautious. I need to show her that I have changed. I am willing to go the distance this time and prioritize her. Not work, not whatever stressor is threatening to bring me down, not distance.

Part of me is tempted to push further, to convince her to give us a chance, to explore what could be between us. There's a sense of urgency and desire, a longing that has been buried deep within me for years. And I'm not accustomed to being on the other side of such negotiations. But Hollis keeps drawing me in, making me want to fight for and build our shared connection.

Yet, I'm also keenly aware of the fine line between persistence and respect. Hollis has her reasons for apprehension, and her boundaries should be honored. There's a uniqueness about her that defies the usual dynamics. And a sign to me that she and this are different.

I finally feel like I'm in a place where I can receive her and be the man she deserves. Before, I wasn't ready to settle down. I can't explain it or even understand it myself, but I finally truly feel ready to settle down and commit to someone. To Hollis.

I want to touch her face but don't want to wake her. I've already done that once today. She needs her rest. So I enjoy the view of her, watching her chest rise and fall. A light strand of hair bisects her face, and I desperately want to move it for her, but I abstain.

She rolls over, placing her arm around my waist. She is undoubtedly relaxed. I hope that the apprehension I sensed earlier has subsided just enough for her to let me show her how I will take care of her.

Her head nestles into my chest, and her arm that is draped over me squeezes me tight.

"What time is it? I can't believe I fell asleep so hard."

"It is almost 2:30. We both conked out. I just woke up, too, but I have spent the last ten minutes watching you, marveling at your beauty."

"Mmmm. You make sleeping so fun," she says with a smile, and she draws herself back, allowing me to see that pretty face again.

"You still hungry for lunch? We messed up on that one. We can still walk down there if you are. I know I need something!"

"Yes! You made me work up an appetite. I worked so hard that I had to take a nap. Let's get something to eat. It will just take me a few minutes to freshen up."

Just as she says that, I hear the slow, familiar walk of Mr. Bojangles down the hall. He must hear us talking and know we are now awake.

"I'll take Mr. B out while you get dressed. Take your time."

"You're amazing. Thank you. I won't be long."

6:24 PM *EST*

WE'VE HAD a full day of just the two of us. Well, three of us, mostly. She doesn't go far or many places without him. Rather than turning me off or me growing impatient, it has done the opposite. I can't get enough of her. Or him, for that matter.

She walks out to the living room, her hair wet from a shower. She is wearing loose-fitting jeans and a soft blue linen button-down shirt. I've never seen a more beautiful sight. I'm excited to share this pleasant evening with her.

It's around 6:30, and I am putting together a little charcu-terie board. When I asked Olivier to shop for breakfast, I also asked him to pick out a few good cheeses, crackers, and some deli meats. I have no clue what I am doing, but I love a good cheese board, so I am throwing it all on there as best I can. No matter how it looks, it will still hit the spot with a big glass of pinot noir.

I can tell she is disappointed that she and her mother have missed each other a few times today. I feel partly to blame for that and want to make it right. They are at the movies but are due to get out any minute. She has her phone in hand, awaiting their call.

"After you talk to Reeves, do you want to sit on the deck and enjoy the sky fading to dark with me? I'm sure you've seen it a thousand times, but you've never seen it with me," I say with a pathetic grin. Her barriers seem to have soft-ened, but I still worry that I will come on too strong.?

"I would love that. Let me dry my hair and talk to Reeves, and I will be right out."

She walks back down the hall. I put the finishing touches on my board by throwing some almonds in there. They hit the wood plate with a clink. It doesn't look like a pro job. I am quite pleased with myself, regardless.

I open a bottle of wine and reach for two large bowl wine glasses, the thin crystal bases singing as they meet with the granite countertop. My heart beats with excitement, antici-pating sharing this time with Hollis.

I carefully carry my labor of love, the cheese and meat board, to the deck and return for the wine bottle and the two glasses. Once I have everything set up, she comes out. Her hair is smooth and light, the regular soft curls brushed out, leaving it straight and silky. Her fine hair flows with the evening breeze.

The weather is perfect. It is just the right amount of warmth to not be cold, but the humidity and hot heat ceased as soon as the sun started making its way down.

The overcast clouds left long ago, and the sky is clear. Streaks of orange and pink and purple are painted across as far as the eye can see.

On this side, we don't get to see the sun dipping into the ocean, but the sky puts on the most beautiful picture show of colors. It is my favorite thing to do here, and I'm excited to share it with her.

She walks out to the deck, her hair dry and pulled back.

"Were you able to catch Reeves and Crazy Roberta?"

"I was. They only had a few minutes in between the movie and dinner. But that was enough. I just needed to hear his voice."

My heart swells at how dedicated she is to her son.

"Can I offer you a glass of pinot noir?"

"That would be wonderful, thank you. It is a perfect night for a glass of wine and an art show in the sky. And look at you. That cheese board looks like a professional put it together."

I beam with pride. She is probably just being nice, but it makes me feel good that she noticed. I stand up to pour the wine and place the cheese board between us on the small side table. I hand her the glass and pour my own.

"To new beginnings."

"To new beginnings," she says back as I lean in to kiss her. I melt in the seat, overcome with emotion. I have so many words I want to say but don't know how to string them into coherent sentences. So I take a sip and choose not to say anything right now. I soak it all up, drinking in the moment.

I can't put my finger on it, but something in her eyes feels out of reach. A change from only a moment ago. Is it something I said? I start to ask but decide to let it go for now.

"Grayson, I have something I want to talk to you about. Something you should know before this goes any further."

It's one of those moments in the movies when everything seems perfect, the music queued to reflect everyone's feelings. And then the sound of the needle on the record as the music stops.

My stomach drops. Her face looks serious. I have no idea what she is about to say, but something tells me she isn't about to suggest we go back inside for round two.

THIRTY-EIGHT

Hollis

_____

7:02 pm EST

THE ANTICIPATION GNAWS at me as I prepare myself to share the secret I've guarded so closely for years. That Reeves, my son, is also his son. I've grappled with this for years, thinking that since I missed that crucial window before he was born to tell him, and since we live on opposite ends of the country, that I would deal with it when I had to.

The time has come.

I never expected all of this. Grayson has been so earnest and kind, showering me with attention and care. It was almost easier when he didn't have the time of day for me. I thought about him like this the whole time, and I yearned for something more. And now that I have it, this secret between us is gnawing at me more than ever.

As I sit here, the calming ocean in front of me, I feel anything but calm. I know I have alarmed him by saying I need to talk to him. He is quietly waiting for me to follow through. We are both silent as I gather the courage.

This won't survive on an unsure footing. I have to come clean. The longer this goes on without me being honest, the worse I am for it. I have been making excuses and shoving it down for far too long. There are no new beginnings without knowing the truth, which is a barrier between us.

My mind races with thoughts of how to start. How do I reveal the existence of a child that he knows nothing about? Rather, he is fully aware of the child and has even met him. He just doesn't know that Reeves is his.

The sound of a truck engine barreling down the sand on the beach draws my attention, giving my nerves a momentary lapse. I catch sight of Grayson's silhouette as he looks across me at the source of the foreign sound. My heart quickens its pace, and my palms grow moist with nerves. The moment of reckoning has arrived.

"So…" I say, my voice trembling ever so slightly. My heart is literally beating out of my chest. "I've been keeping a secret."

Silence. I guess I expected a response to give me a clue as to how to respond. But realistically, what does someone say to that kind of proclamation? I can only imagine what types of scenarios he could be conjuring about a secret I could be keeping that would have any relevance to him and a possible relationship between us.

Grayson clears his throat, breaking the silence that stretches between us. "Hollis, I want you to know that I meant everything I said to you. But I also know this is a lot and fast. I am sure there are lots of things for both of us that we will learn. I don't want to rush anything, but I also don't want to miss an opportunity to explore this between us like I did before. There is nothing you can say that will convince me that we shouldn't give this a try. How that looks and progresses, I will leave it up to you."

He just keeps surprising me. His words make me start to cry. I don't know what I am crying for but can't stop. The fact that I never told him. The fact that I have done all of this on my own for all of these years. The fact that I've dreamed of this moment with him, and it is finally here. The fear that when I tell him, he may reject me or, worse, my son. Maybe it is all of these things.

"I'm so sorry. Please don't cry. I promise, whatever you say is not as bad as you think. I am not going anywhere."

His words sting. I want to believe him, but he has no idea how profound this secret is. I find myself torn between the relief of his acknowledgment and the weight of my own deceit. It's now or never. I need to tell him about Reeves.

"Grayson, it's Reeves," I say, my voice steady despite the turmoil inside me. I pause, trying not to let my words get ahead of my thoughts.

His expression shifts to a mixture of concern and curiosity. "I will love Reeves as my own. You don't have to worry about that."

I take a deep breath, my eyes locked onto him, and the words tumble out of me. "Reeves, my son, is your son. You're his father."

Grayson's eyes widen in disbelief, his gaze fixed on me as though he's just been struck by a lightning bolt. A heavy silence hangs between us for a moment, the weight of my revelation sinking in. Then, with an equal measure of shock, curiosity, and a hint of emotion I can't quite decipher, he finally speaks.

"Reeves... is my son?" He utters, his voice barely more than a whisper.

I nod, my heart pounding in my chest. Tears are rolling down my cheeks. A breath catches in my throat. "Yes. Reeves is your son, Grayson. I should have told you a long time ago, but I was scared and didn't know how to reach out to you. I didn't want to disrupt your life. Things were so fleeting between us, and when we did communicate, it was so brief. I just didn't know how to do it."

Grayson's expression remains a complex mix of emotions, a storm of thoughts churning beneath the surface. "I can't believe it," he says, his voice shaky. "I didn't know what I expected you to say, but I never imagined in a hundred years that it would be this."

"It was a difficult time for both of us back then," I explain, my voice trembling with emotion. "I thought it was the best decision at the time, and then as time went on, it only made it harder and more awkward. I should have told you, and I'm sorry for keeping it from you."

He takes a moment to process the enormity of what I've revealed. "Reeves... I thought that time had passed for me. To have a child."

Tears well up in my eyes as I respond, "I understand this is a lot to take in, Grayson. I don't expect you to have all the answers right now, but I wanted you to know the truth before either of us invested any more."

I don't say it, and now certainly isn't the time, but I hope one day he and Reeves will have a relationship. That Reeves will know his father and that Grayson will know his son.

Grayson rubs his temples, his brows furrowed as he contemplates everything I've said. "I need time to process this, Hollis. I don't know what to say right now."

I nod in understanding. Of course. I wouldn't expect anything less. I'll answer any questions you have if you have any at all."

We sit silently for a while, the weight of our conversation still thick and uncomfortable. The future is uncertain, and many challenges are ahead, but the weight is finally lifted from my shoulders. The truth is out. Let fate be what it may.

There is a part of me that is sad. I may well have derailed what could have been, but if that is the case, then it isn't meant to be for us in the first place. But that doesn't mean it has to end there for Grayson and Reeves.

I swallow hard, the words suspended in the air. Grayson gets up and paces up and down the length of the extended deck. I feel awkward like I shouldn't be here now. I could easily walk home from here. I am at a loss for the best way to support him in this.

The air is charged with the complex circumstances and emotions that bind us.

With a heavy heart and a mix of emotions swirling within me, I gather the courage to speak the words that have been echoing in my mind. "Grayson, I think it's best if I go."

It's a painful proclamation, and part of me wishes I could utter different words. Or that he would tell me not to leave. But whichever way this goes, I think he needs some space. I am an intruder here right now.

As I look into his eyes, I see a flicker of disappointment and a trace of understanding. It's evident that he's caught in the same web of emotions as I am, pulled between the taste of what we have shared and discovered about each other over the last day and a half and the fear of how quickly it is all getting so real.

I hold his gaze for a moment longer, wishing the circumstances were different. That our shared history was less complicated. But the weight of our past decisions, the unspoken words that kept us apart, had to be addressed to move forward.

I walk inside, and he doesn't stop me. That is for the best. I probably wouldn't have the strength to protest. And it is evident to me now that he needs some time.

As I walk through the sliding glass door, over the threshold that just a few hours ago was the start of our explosive union, I wince at the thought of what could have been. A part of me aches with the knowledge that I may be pushing him away. If I had the stomach to sit there while he paces and remains silent, maybe we could come through stronger on the other side.

I gather my things and stuff them into my bag. "Come on, Buddy," I say in my most cheerful voice, encouraging Mr. Bojangles to follow me. He comes willingly. He would follow me into a fire if I were headed there. My constant companion.

The door closes behind me, and I'm left alone with my thoughts. As I descend the front steps, the gnawing feeling of having been here before strikes me. History repeating itself.

It is dark now as we walk down the quiet neighborhood streets. I am grateful that, at this time, no cars are whizzing past us. The solitude is comforting.

I can't believe it hasn't even been twenty-four hours since the accident. It feels like another lifetime.

————

TUESDAY, *August 15th*

12:47 *am EST*

I'M LEFT ALONE in the quiet of my home, the quietest I think it has ever been. My thoughts and emotions swirl through me like a hurricane. It's well past midnight, and the world outside my window is cloaked in the stillness of the night. The room feels both too small and too vast, and I'm acutely aware of the emptiness that is all around me.

Nervous energy courses through my veins. Doubt that I handled it properly creeps in. And shame for letting it get as far as I did without telling him. All of these emotions leave me feeling like a tightrope walker, teetering on the edge of stability, cursing myself for possibly losing the first real connection with a man I have ever felt.

The weight of the secret being lifted is now replaced, and I'm left to grapple with the magnitude of him knowing the truth and with my own fears of rejection. Again.

I long to reach out to Kendall, but it's too late to burden her. I have been leaning on her too much the last few days, these last few years, truth be told.

And here I thought we were finally through the worst of it. Instead, I'm right back into the thick of it. I'm confined to the solitude of my thoughts. I'm alone like I have been my whole life.

The room bears the scent of the white linen candle I lit earlier. It is my favorite, and I thought it would create some normalcy. Instead, its soft flash only serves to cast dancing shadows across the walls, accentuating the anxiety I am feeling. I walk over to the driftwood table, where it flickers, and blow it out.

I sit in the dimly lit space on my infinite, lonely sofa, my knees drawn to my chest. I know I should go to bed. Sitting here in the dark feeling sorry for myself isn't helpful to anyone.

————

7:07 am EST

I'M SETTLED in my usual spot at the front of Sacred Grounds. I needed to get out of that quiet house. I think I am operating on about three hours of sleep, but I tend to write some of my best stuff under those circumstances.

I've decided to let my tragedy fuel me.

My focus shifts to my new book, *Whispers in the Tides*. I've been having writer's block, so I put it down for a bit. I will use this angst and free time to dig back in.

I could learn a thing or two from my protagonist, Lily, who is a single mom grappling with the fragility of human connections and the enduring power of hope. She is the strong female that I hope to be one day. In the thick of it, sometimes I lose sight of that.

The familiar aroma of freshly brewed coffee fills my lungs, wrapping around me like a warm embrace. The gentle hum of conversation and the soft jazz playing in the background provide me with just the right amount of noise to turn off the chatter in my head.

Kendall isn't working today. It's still too early to call, so I will have to fill her in at some point today. Frankly, I don't have the energy right now.

I got to FaceTime with Reeves on my walk down here. He is the one human I knew would be up with the roosters like me. He is having a great time with G-mom and Pops. They have already visited the Children's Museum, the Aquarium, and the splash pad. And he has only been there two full days.

My mom has more energy than I do. This is good for them and Reeves. And for me, for that matter.

My laptop is open, the little vertical line at the start of a new chapter blinking at me, telling me to get cracking. Mr. Bojangles lounges at my feet, his soft fur brushing against my foot. His head is down, but his eyes watch everyone coming and going.

My latte, a dark roast with a hint of hazelnut, is steaming in my favorite mug. Its rich aroma mingles with the earthy scents of this old space. All of the scents in here bring me comfort. I can feel the warmth travel down my chest, into my stomach, and continuing to my toes. The first sip is always the best. I savor every drop. A respite from the complexities of my life.

The round wooden table, now affectionately known as "Hollis's Hangout," is etched with the scars of countless coffee cups and the occasional spills over the years. It's worn and smooth to the touch, bearing witness to the many stories that have unfolded upon its surface, many before I even sat here. If these walls could talk.

I place my fingers on the keyboard, ready to make the blinking line produce sentences and stories. The clacking of the keys punctuates the murmured conversations all around me.

As soon as I start, everything and everyone else fades away. The ambient noise, a blend of soft laughter, hushed discussions, and the occasional clink of porcelain against a saucer, is a soothing backdrop to my thoughts.

As I work, a sense of peace covers me, and I feel I am finally reclaiming a semblance of control over my life. Reeves is with my mother, and I'm getting back to my writing.

I'm lost in the rhythm of my typing, the words on my screen flowing from my fingertips, when I sense a subtle shift in the atmosphere around me. It's as if a gentle breeze has swept through the café, causing the ambient sounds to hush briefly. My heart quickens, and I can't help but look up.

It's a feeling that touches my skin and makes the back of my neck prickle. My eyes dart around, scanning the familiar surroundings, searching for what has disrupted my peaceful solitude. And then I see him.

Grayson Sterling is standing near the entrance, bathed in the soft glow of the café's amber lighting. He hasn't noticed me yet. His attention is fixed on the menu board as he contemplates his order. His presence fills the room, commanding attention with his stature and ridiculously handsome good looks.

Mr. Bojangles notices him, too. He lifts his head, his ears turned on high alert. He watches him intently. It isn't lost on me that we are both waiting on a sign from him. I look back down at my computer, not wanting to create an awkwardness if he isn't interested in speaking to me.

Just yesterday morning, he was here with Mr. Bojangles, buying me a latte. Now, here I sit, looking down to avoid eye contact. My, how quickly things can change.

Back to Lily. She discovers her small town home has a secret. As she delves more into the mysterious disappearances that seem to happen there every three years, like clockwork, she realizes some very powerful people are working to keep the details hidden. And then she discovers why.

"Good morning, beautiful," his deep, rough voice says as he slides in beside me on the bench seat. I am started at first, but one whiff of his familiar bergamot and sandalwood cologne and any nervousness evaporates. I wonder if he can see the lump that has formed in my throat at the sight of him.

"Well, hello there. You sure are chipper this morning." I want to tell him how handsome he is, but I am not sure where we are at the moment. The fact that he slid in beside me and his firm thigh is touching mine is a good sign.

"I am chipper because I was hoping to find you here, and I have. I missed you last night. I am sorry I went into my silent imaginary bunker yesterday evening. It is no reflection on you or that precious boy of yours." He clears his throat and corrects himself. Semantics. "Of ours. I didn't see that coming, so it took me some time to work through it."

"Understandable. You do not have to apologize at all. I am glad you recognized your need to do that and took the time. That takes strength. I admire you for that."

"I feel like such an idiot that I didn't put the pieces together the minute I saw you guys on the beach. I'm like the biggest fucking idiot. Sorry about that. I am working on my language, too. But, duh! His age, his hair, and blue eyes, for crying out loud."

I laugh. Because it is true. Reeves is a complete mini-me of Grayson. I don't see much of myself in him, except maybe his stubbornness.

But most people don't imagine that someone is keeping the paternity of a child from his father, so I get it. "Look, I get it. Why would you even think that? I apologize for not telling you immediately. I have felt terrible since. I hope you will forgive me."

He puts his hand on my thigh and squeezes. "Forgive you? Hell, I want to thank you. When I tell you that period in my life and the eighteen months that followed was a a complete mess, I am not exaggerating."

He clears his throat, seemingly fighting back becoming emotional. I want to hold him and let him know that I feel him. But I can see he has more to say, so I resist letting him finish.

"I hate that you did this alone, and I would do anything now to go back in time to help you. But if I'm being completely honest with you and myself, I fear things could have turned out completely differently between us if you had. And I am hoping you will still give me, give us, another chance. So, what do you say?"

"Grayson, what exactly are you asking me?" I ask with a smile, giving him a hard time, but I am also legitimately unsure if I am hearing this correctly. Things are getting a bit serious this early in the morning.

"I'm apologizing, thanking you for the space you gave me, and asking if you're willing to take a gamble on this old, foul-mouthed, commitment-adverse, work-a-holic? Should I put it in writing and slip you a note instead?"

He smiles and leans his head on my shoulder. Mr. Bojangles is resting his head on Grayson's knee, watching us as if he is waiting with bated breath to hear my answer.

"Of course I will. I am grateful you still want to try this with me and your ready-made family."

"This is a gift, Hollis. You have given me a gift. I never thought I wanted children until very recently. I have noticed all my friends with their families and children getting older. And I wanted that for the first time but figured that ship had sailed. There was never anyone I could even imagine myself starting a family with. Until you."

"I am officially speechless. Thank you for your thoughtfulness. And thank you for finding me. You have a knack for jumping in right when I start to feel like I am getting on solid footing. That is a good thing. You're good for me, Grayson Sterling."

He leans in and plants one on me, right here in Sacred Grounds. My sacred ground. I find myself getting way into it for being in public, but dammit, I feel like I deserve a little PDA right now. I put my hand on the back of his head and don't let him away, drawing out the kiss just a few seconds longer.

"Hollis, there's something else." Oh, God, I think to myself. What possibly more could either of us spring on each other now?

"I'd like to ask if you and Reeves, if he will be back in time, would like to come with me to my ribbon cutting next week. It's a big deal, and I will be honored for my contribution and involvement in this project. I have been working on it since we first met, so it is perfect timing that it's happening now, just as we are coming back together. And I would like for the two of you to be there."

I am honored he would want us there. I know this will be a big step as we will essentially be going as a family. "Of course we will. What is the date? Reeves is coming back on Saturday."

"Perfect. It is Sunday. It will be like a fair, with ponies, clowns, hayrides, and food trucks. It will be much more enjoyable with you both by my side."

Grayson's face lights up, and he looks genuinely pleased. "Fuck, yeah! It's going to be an unforgettable day."

I give him a look.

His eyes widen, and his lips part, spreading in an exaggerated smile that stretches across his face.

"Sorry, I will have my mouth cleaned up by Saturday. Promise."

THIRTY-NINE

Grayson

Saturday, August 19th

1:01 PM *EST*

IT'S a perfect late August Saturday. The weather at the beach is sunny and mild. The afternoons are hot, but the mornings and the evenings are starting to be cooler, letting us know that the fall, while still a long way off, is on the way.

The weather in L.A. rarely varies. It is a little less humid there but always hot during the day. We might get an occasional cooler day in January or February, but there aren't significant changes in the temperature. It's either no rain for weeks at a time in the summer or wet winters. That is how I mark the season changes there.

Hollis and Mr. Bojangles have been staying with me all week, and it has been amazing. She is helping me cuss less, preparing me for Reeves' arrival today. Plus, she is outstanding in the bedroom, so we have been practicing our skills in that department, which has been out of this world.

I've had to get on a few calls, but for the most part, I have been off the grid. I've worked hard my whole life and have a net worth of over four billion dollars. I think I can sit back and enjoy the fruits of my labors.

I'll never quit working. I love it too much. But I don't have to be married to it, living only for the next deal or development opportunity. My company can continue to do its job. I have a hundred and fifty employees, after all.

Reeves should get back in town around five today. Hollis invited her parents to stay the night, offering to get a sitter and go to dinner at Cafe Pamlico. But they really want to get back home. Based on what Hollis says, her mom has been running hard daily with Reeves, and a week with a little one when you aren't used to it can be exhausting. Hell, a day with a high-energy boy will wipe out anyone.

The thought of this new change is terrifying. I know I can learn the ropes, and we will be fine. But I have no idea what to do with a kid. I don't even know how to talk to children.

So Hollis's parents will be in and out, arriving in about four hours. They plan to drive halfway and stay in a small town called Rocky Mount for the night, so they only have about three hours to go when they wake up tomorrow.

Hollis wants me to meet them, so I plan to be there when they arrive. I don't love the idea of experiencing my son for the first time with the knowledge that he is my son in front of strangers, but what will you do?

Hollis said she has no plans to tell them right now, so hopefully, they will be as imperceptive as I was when they see the resemblance.

We are heading to lunch now. Olivier is pulling into The Sanderling. Hollis became close to the folks at the restaurant here when she lived here all those years ago after the fire.

She has created a little makeshift family for herself with people up and down the island. I can see how important all of these people are to her and that they have played an essential role in supporting her and helping her with Reeves after he was born.

I am looking forward to meeting some of them today.

"I know this restaurant isn't your typical choice, so I want you to know I appreciate you going with me. I am excited to show you off to some of the people here who really took care of me when I lived here. They are going to love you."

"This is totally my kind of restaurant. What are you even talking about? Any place that is your place is my choice. I'm excited because I get to be your plus one."

Once we are at the front door, Olivier puts the Range Rover in park and walks around to Hollis's side to open her door. She is already opening it by the time he arrives, so he holds it open for her, even though it isn't necessary, while she gets out. She is still not entirely comfortable with being taken around town by a driver.

We walk through the main doors and head to Lifesaving Station No. 5. It is a southern meat-and-potato type of place with a seafood twist. I'm looking forward to some fried popcorn shrimp and collards. It's a perfect combo.

"My mom just texted, and they are a little ahead of schedule. She thinks they will get here a little after four. Are you still good to come by the house to meet them?"

"Of course. I wouldn't miss it for the world," I say, which is true. I wouldn't miss it. But I don't tell her I am incredibly nervous about the whole thing. My stomach has been hurting all morning, and I know that is why. I feel like I'm fourteen all over again, meeting my prom date's dad.

"You know they are going to love you, right? Just make sure to watch your mouth." She winks at me and doesn't skip a beat. "They probably won't stay long, so you should be able to manage that, right?" She smiles, poking me in the side as she does.

It's not the swear words I am worried about. It's meeting my almost five-year-old son for the first time. I don't count that day on the beach because I barely said six words to him. And I think he said even less. I was more focused on his mom at that point.

But now I know. I am sure I will see him in a whole new light. I have become so emotional these days. I just hope I can keep it together. I also don't want to give it away to her parents that this is our first encounter as father and son.

FORTY

Hollis

4:34 pm EST

"MY LITTLE MAN," I yell as I run out to the Rav-4 as it pulls into the driveway. "I have missed you so much! Did you have a great time with G-mom and Pops?"

His big smile fills me. He holds out a little plastic and cardboard llama figure to me when I let his hug go. I start to unbuckle his harness but then stop to inspect the figure. "What is this?"

"His name is Lloyd. He is the llama from a story that G-mom reads to me every night. He loves his llama momma, just like me."

I fight tears as I finish taking off his five-point harness. Reeves jumps out of the car and makes a dash straight to Mr. Bojangles, who is standing just back from the car, waiting for his greeting.

"Hi, Mom. You're a saint. Are you exhausted?"

She laughs and says, "He definitely has a lot of energy. Your dad and I loved having him so much. Thank you for this time with him. I know you missed him, but we will treasure this forever."

"It was a good break for me, too. I needed it more than I realized. Mom, I want you to meet someone."

By this time, my dad is already out and talking to Grayson. Two men drawn to each other like magnets.

"This is my friend, Grayson Sterling. Grayson, this is my mom, Roberta Greer. It looks like you have already met my dad, Bobby."

I just introduced Grayson as my friend. I don't know how to define what we are. Maybe "Baby Daddy" would have been more appropriate.

Grayson reaches out his hand to my mom, "Hi, Mrs. Greer. It is so nice to meet you. I have heard so many great things about you and Mr. Greer. You survived a nine-hour trip on the road with a four-year-old, so I know you have just as much grit as your daughter. Bravo."

"It's nice to meet you, Grayson," my mom says, giving me the side eye. "Do you live here on the island?"

I know he can be modest about what he does. I am curious to see how he navigates this minefield.

"I have a house less than a mile from here. My home base is in California, but I spend a fair amount of time here." That isn't exactly true, but maybe he is projecting for the future. Regardless, I get butterflies in my stomach watching him interact with my parents.

Reeves tugs at my shorts, and I kneel down to his level. "What is it, sweet love? Are you happy to be home with your buddy? Did you miss Mr. Bojangles?"

He nods his head, exaggerating the motion. "Can I have a snack, please?"

"Your manners are so good. You make Mommy so proud. Of course, you can." I stand up to let the other adults know I am taking him in.

"Mom, Dad. Do y'all want to come in for a potty break or something to drink? Reeves wants a snack, so we will go inside to get him something."

My mom accepted the offer, and my dad declined. "We need to get on the road, Honey if we are going to get to Rocky Mount before dark. Don't go in there and get stuck. Do your business, and let's get going."

Dad is still the drill sergeant, keeping us all on track. I am secretly relieved. It means she won't have time to drill me, which I know she wants to.

"Alright, Mom. You heard him. Let's get in there for a pitstop bathroom break." She puts her arm in mine, and we walk in together. The four of us, of course, are me, Mom, Reeves, and Mr. Bojangles. He and Reeves will be attached for the next several days for sure.

Grayson stays out talking to my dad about golf.

"Okay, what is the deal with Mr. Handsome Face out there? Is he really just a friend?"

"We are exploring it. We actually met years ago," I am careful not to divulge the exact number of years ago. "We hit it off then, but he was working a lot and traveling all over the world, so it didn't work."

Justifying it out loud does make sense. I just wish there had been more communication between us that morning. I digress.

"He has been here all week, so we have done dinner and some walks on the beach, just getting to know each other again."

"Any chance you met about five years ago, hmm?" Dammit. My mom is good. I knew she would pick up on it. She never asked me again about Reeves's father when she saw how distraught I was about the whole situation. I told her we weren't in contact, and she let it go.

"Mom, let's not talk about it right now. I'll explain more in detail later. Okay?" I ask, looking at her with raised eyebrows. She smiles, letting me know I have already told her everything she needs to know. I get my love of solving mysteries from her. She could rival Olivia Benton any day.

"Okay, let's see what we can find for you. I have hummus and carrots. I have gummies. I have veggie straws. What are you feeling like?"

"Straws!" His face lights up. He looks like he grew an inch in a week. I pull him to me and give him another big hug.

"I sure missed you." I let him go as he is already trying to wiggle out of my grasp. I go to the pantry and pull out the bag of veggie straws. I pour a portion into a plastic bowl and set it on the table.

"I'm a big boy now. I can sit in this chair," he says, hitting the side of the chair with the palm of his hand. I can see we got some new privileges with the grandparents this week.

"You are a big boy. If you can sit still at mealtime, we can make that happen. But if you're in a big boy's chair, you must sit like a big boy. Can you do that?"

"He sure can," my mom answers from behind me as she walks up. "He sat in a big boy chair for every meal and did great. We only spilled our cereal one time. He is such a sweet boy, Hollis. I can't tell you enough how much we enjoyed having him. I hope we can make this an annual thing. Camp Pops, right Reeves?"

Reeves nods his head, again exaggeratingly so. He has several straws in his mouth, his cheeks pushed out like a chipmunk.

"Walk me out, Hollis. Your dad is probably chomping at the bit, so I need to get out there. Reeves, can I have one more hug? Pops and I have to leave to get back home. I had so much fun with you. I love you."

"I love you, too, G-mom. I want to go to the Aquarium again. I like to see the sharks."

"We will go back for sure when you come back to see us. Maybe next time, your mom will come, too."

"Okay."

"Alright, Bud. I love you so much."

Reeves is not one for long goodbyes. He jumps up and resumes his position in his big boy chair at the table.

I follow Mom back outside to join the boys. As soon as Dad sees us, he shakes Grayson's hand and starts heading for the car, letting us know there is no time for us to join in on the man talk.

"Grayson, it was a pleasure to meet you. Hopefully, we can plan to spend more time with you next time if you'll be in town."

"That would be great," he says genuinely. I can sense the relief on his face that they are leaving. Not necessarily because they are hard to be around, because they are so easy. And their visit was thankfully brief. But because I think he is anxious to spend some time with Reeves.

FORTY-ONE

Grayson

5:54 pm EST

I FLIP the steaks on the grill, check the baked potatoes and corn on the cob on the top rack, and add two hot dogs for Reeves. I'm getting pretty good at this cooking thing.

I've grilled a handful of times, but when it is just me, I find myself mostly eating out or having someone come to the house to do the cooking.

We decided to come to my house to let Reeves get out on the sand before dinner. Hollis says he is going through this stage where he loves going to the beach and exploring for shells, jellyfish, and sand dollars.

I am up on the deck, grilling and watching them as they run around below. Hollis brought a tennis ball for Mr. Bojangles, and he is fetching it just at the water's edge while Reeves is hunched over, looking at something in the sand. I beam with the sense of connection I have never felt before. These are my people.

I am sure of the suspicion now. I fell in love with Hollis years ago, and now, with everything that has happened since then, I am certain. I have never felt like this for another person. I didn't think I had it in me.

The sun is low, but it hasn't set yet. Our evenings are getting shorter, and the sunset is getting a little earlier each day. A gentle breeze is building up behind the still-warm air.

The sky is already showing us a glimpse of what to expect tonight. The pinks and deep oranges are subtly streaking where the water meets the horizon. The colors will become more profound and vibrant as the sun descends behind us. There is nothing quite like watching the sky at the beach as the day turns into night.

So far, so good with Reeves. As is to be expected for a four-year-old, his attention span is short. But we have talked some and are getting to know each other.

He calls me Grayman, which I find pretty endearing. I have no idea where he pulled that one, but it was almost immediate. I think it was probably a mistake at first, but when he saw my reaction, it became a thing. I like it.

I asked him if that meant I should call him Reeveson. He laughed and called me silly. I thought it was pretty clever.

He told me his favorite truck is a firetruck. His favorite sport is kickball. And his best friends are Mr. Bojangles and his mom.

I told him that I build tall buildings, fly on a jet, and live in the city where movies are made. He still can't believe that I help "make skyscrapers" and fly in a plane.

He asked if I knew the president of the United States. I told him I'd met one before but that I didn't know the current one. That was enough to put me in wow status for him. At least for the moment.

Hollis and I talked about this reunion before today. We both agree that we want to tell Reeves that I am his father sooner rather than later, but we don't want to do it today as soon as he got home. We still haven't devised a definite plan, so we are getting to know each other for now and feeling it out.

My suggestion is we tell him after the carnival tomorrow. It will be a long day there, and the ride is a hike, so it may be better to wait until Monday. Whenever it is, and however we will do it, we both agree it will occur before I return to L.A. next weekend. My heart thumps harder and faster at the thought of all of that. The telling him and the leaving him.

I have been smiling uncontrollably since the Greers left. Nothing personal against them. I just did a better job of keeping it at bay while they were still here. I am generally not a prolific smiler, so this is another new sensation for me. But talking to this tiny human, knowing he shares my DNA, has really done a number on me. I had no idea how happy it would make me to know I have a son.

"Grayman! Look what I found." Reeves comes running up the deck towards me. He is holding a shiny, black shark tooth about the size of a nickel in his hand. It is bigger than any I have ever found on this beach. Or any beach, for that matter.

"Wow. That is so cool. How big do you think that shark was?" It is fascinating how black it is. Like the blackest black. Why are shark's teeth black? I've always wondered about this.

"Bigger than this whole house. I think it was probably a Megalodon shark. Those are dinosaur sharks, you know."

"Oh, you think so, huh? Well, you better save that one."

Hollis' head is just becoming visible as she ascends the steps. Mr. Bojangles is a few steps ahead of her, never too far from her side. They both look exhausted based on their slow cadence up.

As her face comes more into focus, I see she is smiling. A tingling sensation, like a soft electrical current, spreads across my skin at the sight of her. As she gets closer, the tingles grow more intense.

I want to kiss her once she is close enough, but I don't know how Reeves might react, so I resist. Most kids at four wouldn't even notice, but I prefer to be cautious at this point. So, I imagine it instead.

She comes directly to me, puts her arm around me, and pulls me to her in a side hug. I will take it. Any chance to feel her body anywhere on mine is a win. I pull her side into mine, holding on for an extra few seconds.

"How was the beach?" I inhale the scent of her hair, drinking it in. It will sustain me for now.

"Fabulous. Reeves was so happy to be out there. I don't know if he can ever live anywhere that's not on the beach now. He is a bonafide beach bum. How about that shark tooth? That thing is legit!"

"It's huge. Did he really find that himself?"

"Yes! He was walking right at the edge of the water, looking at all of the little pieces of shells that congregated there. He has figured out that the shark's teeth shine differently than the other black shells. He tried to explain, but I didn't see it. But he went right to it."

"So cool. Dinner is almost ready. We could sit out here if that works for you? The evening art display in the sky will happen soon, so we will have front-row seats."

"Duh! Of course, we will sit outside. I will go make drinks and get some silverware."

"I'll get everything plated up for us, and we can sit down when you get back. I want to kiss you so badly."

"Well, if you're a big boy at dinner, maybe you will get the chance later…" She walks away as she trails off, her head tilted toward me as she does. She is teasing me. My growing need for her pushes against my pants.

FORTY-TWO

Hollis

Sunday, August 20,

Harbor Vista

Virginia Beach, VA

10:11 *am EST*

WE PULL into the entrance to Harbor Vista at Virginia Beach. With its commanding stone pillars on either side, it feels like we are driving into the Greenbriar. Everything is awe-inspiring and beautifully done. The landscaping is extensive, with tall green, leafy plants in the middle and cascading red, yellow, and purple flowering plants. There are young but still significant trees down the long center entrance road.

I had no idea how massive this whole project had been. I should have guessed, as he said he began working on the plans and the procurement in 2018, and it is just now finished.

We allowed Reeves to watch *Sing 2* on the television screen in the car for the ride. He was so excited since I don't have screens in my car, and I typically don't allow him to watch an iPad. He kept telling me that he didn't even know that it was possible to watch a movie in the car.

He is a little sleepy, but he will perk up once he sees all of the festivities. He usually takes a nap around midday, but I am phasing that out because he starts school in September and will be there until 2:30 every day.

Olivier drives to the development's community center, the central plaza, as Grayson describes it. It is adorned with fresh flowers, art installations, and a giant water feature replica of the Cape Henry lighthouse—a mesmerizing blend of Virginia history and artistry. Water cascades down the lighthouse façade in a series of intricate channels, creating a dynamic and visually stunning display. It is quite captivating to watch.

An oversized, intricately designed ribbon stretches across the plaza's main entrance, symbolizing the gateway to a new era in community living. This is where the kick-off will start and where most of the vendors appear to be set up.

There are food trucks, a face-painting station, a pony ride corral, and a band setting up. I even see a few clowns milling about. This is going to be a full-on party.

The main event, which is the ribbon cutting, starts at eleven. There is already a crowd gathering. Grayson insisted on driving us around to highlight some of the unique features he is excited about. There is a full k-12 school on the property, equipped to house eight thousand children. Are there even that many children in the state of Virginia? Holy Toledo.

He assures me there are, and this community alone is projected to have at least six to seven thousand school-aged children once it is fully open. The school property is beautiful and expansive. Three separate areas are all connected: elementary, middle, and high school. It's really impressive.

"Are we there yet?" Reeves whines as he rubs his eyes. His little feet kick up from their dangling position in his car seat. The movie just ended, so the timing is perfect.

"Grayman is showing us his new neighborhood that he built. Look at that cool park right there," I point out the window to a large, open green space with playground equipment on the far side. "Want to come play here later? Look at that big slide!"

"Yes, can we, please? I really want to. Can we go now?"

"We can't right now. Remember, we will watch Grayman use the big scissors and cut the bow. Once he does that, we will make sure you get to play, play, play all day."

"Can I use the big scissors?"

"They might be very heavy. We might have to leave that job to Grayman. But he might let you feel them," I say as I look up to Grayson.

"I think we might be able to arrange something. How about this? Would you like to help me cut the ribbon? We can do it together."

"YES! I want to help you. Yes! Yes! Please, Mommy."

Grayson smiles, and Reeves can barely contain himself. "Are you sure he can come up there with you?"

"Of course. I am the boss." Grayson smiles and puts his arm around my shoulder, pulling me to him.

We drive up to a gated section. Olivier uses a key card at a reader outside of the gate, and it opens up. Once we enter, my jaw hits my knee as it opens up to these massive, intricate homes. Some are still being built, but the few that appear to be completed are breathtaking. Olivier drives all the way down to an expansive wharf.

There are already boats moored, even though the property is still not completed. "There will be a full marina here, complete with a ship store and a small cafe. There is a pool exclusive to this area just on the other side, there. The homeowners can buy boat slips and treat this area as their own yacht club."

"This is so beautiful, Grayson. I know you must be so proud. How much are the homes in this part?"

"The lots start at $400,000, and most of the homes built already are valued between $3-5M. We designed this part to be the premiere waterfront community in Virginia."

Mind blown. Officially. "What about some of the smaller homes we saw when we first drove in?"

"The spec and track homes start at $189,000, but we also have affordable housing that includes a full-service apartment building, with rent for a one bedroom under $1,000 per month. We wanted there to be a place for everyone in this development."

"That is quite the range. I'm guessing logistically that was not an easy feat." I place my hand on his firm thigh, feeling his muscles through his tailored blue suit. He looks so handsome, all suited up. I am used to seeing him in shorts or khakis. It is extra sexy seeing him in this light.

"There were some challenges, for sure. But I was determined to create a mixed-income, all-inclusive community. I had a lot of pushback. I kept plunging forward, and here we are. It is a reality."

I am so proud of him. I learn something new about him every day. I was already aware of his business acumen, and I admit I did a Google search on him more than once over the years. So, I know he has a lot of accolades. Knowing he also has a community-centric goal, bringing in everyone, not just the ultra-wealthy, adds a whole new layer of admiration for this man.

"We better get back to the central plaza, Olivier. Thank you for indulging me with my brag tour for Hollis."

———

11:39 *am EST*

GRAYSON AND REEVES are standing together on the large front porch of the commercial spaces that encircle the fountain. There are living space condos above the stores and cafes and restaurants that are housed below.

Watching them both standing there, remarkably similar looking, I am filled with the warmest sense of pride. Hearing all the wonderful things being said about Grayson is genuinely remarkable. He is kind of a big deal, I am realizing. The fact that he is so humble with me says a lot about the type of man he is.

The mayor is walking to the podium to speak.

"Grayson Sterling, the visionary behind Harbor Vista, stands at the forefront, flanked by architects, city planners, and the myriad of professionals who contributed to the development's success. It has been a collaborative effort that went into making Harbor Vista a reality. I would like to take this opportunity to commend Grayson for his commitment to innovation, urban development, and philanthropy."

Applause rings out all around. They are clapping for my man. My handsome, hardworking man who had a dream and didn't stop until it became a reality. I am clapping so hard that my palms sting.

"National publications have hailed Harbor Vista as a groundbreaking example of urban planning. Its strategic location near three major thoroughfares ensures easy access to the entire tri-county area. The development is not just a collection of structures but a vision of sustainable, community-centric living."

More clapping, a few cat-calls. The energy is off the charts.

"As the mastermind behind the project, Mr. Sterling conceived the innovative plan and secured the funding needed to turn the vision into reality. His commitment to creating a diverse, self-sufficient community sets a new gold standard for urban and rural-adjacent developments nationwide."

The mayor motions for Grayson to stand beside him.

"On behalf of Virginia Beach and the state of Virginia, we present you with a key to our city. Let's cut that ribbon!"

Grayson and Reeves, along with the governor and a few other men and women I am sure are important, wield those comically large scissors and cut through the giant red ribbon.

As the two strips fall, the scissors are removed, and Grayson bends down to pick up Reeves. They pose for the flashes and clicks, with several media companies present to capture the moment. Reeves lifts his fist high, not understanding the moment's gravity but excited to be there and in the limelight.

I can't even hold back the tears. I am so proud and grateful for this moment and the fact that we could all be here together. I want to support Grayson and experience such a momentous occasion in his life and career. His son is with him. This will be a day we all will remember for the rest of our lives.

FORTY-THREE

Grayson

7 Allgood Road

Duck, NC

7:32 PM *EST*

THE QUIET LIVING room is a welcome change from our busy day. Hollis has a candle burning and a hot chai tea in hand as she sits cross-legged on the sofa, a book resting on her leg. We had dinner before leaving Virginia Beach.

I am staying here with them tonight. Hollis says she wants Reeves to sleep in his own bed since they stayed at the beach house last night. We have decided that we are going to tell Reeves tomorrow that I am his father. We will leave it up to him to decide if he wants to call me Dad or if he wants to keep calling me Grayman, which I am totally fine with.

For some reason, starting at an early age, I called my dad by his first name. I don't know if that was his request or I just started doing it. He was always just Richard to me.

Children are so resilient and adaptable. I have a hunch it will not be as significant to him right now as it will be for us. And that is the way I want it. I mainly just want him to know what I am to him and that he will be seeing more of me going forward.

Reeves is finally in bed and out like a rock. He was sleeping hard in the car, so I carried him in and put him in the bed. When that didn't wake him, Hollis started changing his clothes into his pajamas and he came out of his slumber for long enough to tell her to leave him alone.

She managed to wake him enough to get him to go to the restroom and brush his teeth. He wasn't happy about it, but he eventually conceded once he realized the fastest way to get her to leave him alone was to comply.

We didn't leave Harbor Vista until almost five this afternoon. It was a fun, full day. Being social is a lot of work. I loved having them there with me and especially for Reeves to be able to be a part of it. It was really special to have him on the stage with me while I cut the ribbon and got the key to the city. He told me he wants to hang it on his wall.

I am still on cloud nine. We rubbed elbows with important people. What I enjoyed most, though, was meeting some of the families already living there or waiting on the finishing touches of their new homes.

So many people approached me and expressed their happiness with Harbor Vista. Even people who won't be living in the community are delighted with the development, which is rare for a big project like this. People are just excited about everything it has already done for their city. The common area spaces and businesses are now accessible to everyone. That was the point.

"It feels good to be back here with you, to get you all to myself," Hollis says as I walk back into the living room. I changed out of my tie and suit, opting for a pair of soft joggers and a black t-shirt. It is taking every ounce of self-restraint not to jump on her. She looks so perfect, snuggled up on the sofa, book in hand.

"Thank you for coming today and for letting Reeves come. It meant the world to have you by my side." She sets her book down on the coffee table and stands up to greet me.

I pull her face to mine and kiss her. She wraps her arms around me, puts her hands on my butt, and pulls me to her. Maybe I should have jumped on her after all. The touch of her body on mine is sending shockwaves through me.

"It was a true honor to be there with you," she says into my chest. I kiss the top of her head while smoothing her hair. "I am glad you invited us and wanted us there. I know Reeves had an amazing time, too. As evidenced by the fact that he fell asleep in the car within about twenty minutes on the road."

I have been thinking about this all week. The day I saw her on the beach, even. I have an undeniable urge to tell her. After today, I can't hold it in any longer.

"Hollis, there is something that I have been wanting to tell you, but I have held it back."

Her eyes soften. She lets go of me and looks at me, ready for me to spill my heart to hear.

"Hollis, I love you. I have been in love with you for years. I just didn't know how to manage it. So, I locked you out. But I never want to be without you again."

She doesn't respond at first. She puts her arms around me, burying her head in me. And then she pulls herself away from me, looking me in the eyes.

"I feel the same way, Grayson. I knew there was something special about you that first day. Well, not immediately upon meeting you. I mean, after you yelled curse words at me and my dog and demanded I be arrested, and Mr. Bojangles put down," I laugh, fond now of that memory. "I love you, too. Not only are you a sexy man on the outside, but you have a heart of gold under that gruff demeanor. I love the man that you are."

I hug her, pulling her head into my chest, wanting my body to swallow hers whole. I close my eyes and let myself sink into her. I am comforted by the rhythm of her breathing, her smell.

For the first time in my life, I feel I am exactly where I need to be with her. For the first time, I feel seen and truly loved. Being with her has always felt right, even before she said the words back to me.

She looks up at me after a moment and stands on her tippy toes. I lean down to her, bringing my mouth to hers. Fireworks inside of me explode as soon as our lips touch. We kiss long and passionately. The one I have been waiting for all day. "How about you take me to bed?" She asks me after we pull apart.

"Hot damn. I can think of nothing else I would rather do."

"Watch your mouth," she says as she takes my hand and leads the way down the short hall to her bedroom.

FORTY-FOUR

Hollis

7:59 pm EST

I TAKE CONTROL. I pull him into my bedroom with a fistful of his shirt. I close the door behind him and turn the lock. He looks at me, eyebrows raised, as if to say he surrenders to me.

He stands there, his bare feet planted on the wood floor in front of the wood six-panel door, his back to the bed.

My thumbs are on either side of his hips, just inside the waistband of his pants, and I slowly slide them down. My nose, barely touching his warm body, follows the pants down. I stick out my tongue and taste his salty skin as I go down.

He is already at full attention, clearly anticipating the congratulations that awaits him.

He steps out of his pants, leaving them right where they fell. A figure eight for him to stand on. I rub his strong legs with my entire palm, feeling his hardness. I place his swollen penis in my mouth, stroking it with my left hand as I slowly bring it in and out of my mouth.

His veiny shaft is hot, the skin as soft as silk. It is large for my mouth, but not prohibitively so. Tasting him, feeling him inside of me in this way, brings me to orgasm before he even touches me.

He taps my shoulder and gently pushes me back. "I am about to come," he says, his head cocked back, a guttural groan coming up from deep inside of him. I stand up, rubbing my hand under his shaft, wrapping my hand around his wet manhood.

I move my hand up and down, ensuring he can finish what I already started. He spasms and lets out a stifled moan. I press myself onto him and hold him for a few minutes, washing myself in his essence. "That was so amazing," he says.

"That was just the appetizer. You ready for the second course?"

I remove his shirt, marveling at the six-pack that he keeps hidden under there shamefully. I rub my hands over it, amazed that the human body can do what his does. I lick his nipple, wanting another taste of him.

"I am always ready for you."

He lifts my shirt over my head. I had already removed my bra, so I pressed my bare breasts on his chest. My hard nipples are extra sensitive, a million nerve endings exploding at the touch of him on them.

The soft, golden glow from a single lamp beside the bed casts an interesting light on his face, highlighting his five o'clock shadow on his chin. The rugged contours and the shadows dancing across his features make me weak at the knees.

I guide him down to the bed. He sits up, his feet planted on the floor, anchoring him. His eyes never leave me, watching my every move, anticipating where I am taking this.

I reach into the drawer beside my bed and get a condom. I open it, the metallic packaging making a slicing noise as I tear it. I take the delicate, slick disc out and kneel down in front of him. He has already restored the blood flow and is ready for his new rain slicker.

I place it on the tip and roll it down, slowly unfolding it with each millimeter. It is snug on him, holding tightly as it becomes a second skin. I trace it up with my pointer finger, lingering at the tip.

Once it is on and is completely unfurled, I use my knees to push his legs closer and straddle him, one foot on either side of him. I place myself directly over his lap and slowly lower myself onto him. And he fills me.

I pull him out and turn around. He is still seated, and I straddle him again, only this time I am facing the same direction. He holds onto me at the top of my hips, helping me position myself over him. He opens his legs, making it easier for me to fit between them. He raises and lowers me, using my hips as handles.

I feel him touching all of the reaches inside of me. I've never been with a man from this position, and it seems I have been missing out. The orgasm that is building inside of me is more intense than anything I have ever felt before. I put my hands on his knees and hold on, about to lose myself. "Grayson, I love you. I love… Grayson. Grayson!"

"I love you too, Hollis. I love you so much, baby."

He pulls me down, holding me still. He wraps his arms around me and hugs me to him, keeping himself inside of me. As we both come down from that epic experience, our two bodies melded into one.

After a few moments I climb off of him. "Will you hold me? I want to fall asleep in your arms."

"It would be my distinct honor."

I pull the covers down and climb into bed. The feel of the cold, smooth sheets on my hot, clammy skin is refreshing. His six-foot-tall frame of pure granite climbs in beside me. He puts his arm under my head, pulling me onto his chest. I could drink him, all of him, right now. I inhale deeply, wanting never to forget this moment, this time together.

My left leg rubs up and down his. Feeling his hair on my skin tickles me, giving me goosebumps. It feels so good, like a sensory-seeking missile on a mission.

I settle in, my left hand positioned on his chest just under the edge of my face. Within moments, I am in a deep sleep, wrapped in safety and love.

————

MONDAY, *August 21st*

6:06 *am EST*

I AM AWAKENED by the softest rap on my bedroom door. It takes me a moment to realize where I am. We have been switching which bed we are staying in the last few nights, and I am momentarily disoriented.

Then I realize that it must be Reeves trying to get in. I forgot that I locked the door when we came to bed, and I forgot to unlock it. And I am thankful I did. We are both nude and in bed together. We still have not discussed any of this with him, so I am not ready to be sleeping in the bed together in front of him, even if he is too young to understand what it all means.

"Good morning, love. I am going to go out and get breakfast ready for Reeves. Stay sleeping as long as you like." I kiss him on the cheek, his eyes still closed. A smile spreads across his face.

"Mmmm. Okay."

I get up and walk to my closet, removing my robe from the door hook. I put it on and tie it tightly.

"Good morning," I say as I open the door and walk into the hall. "You're up bright and early. Is everything okay?" I close the door behind me, leaving a beautiful man behind in my bed.

Mr. Bojangles stretches, his back legs still on his large, canvas dog bed that he sleeps on beside the couch. We are even up before him, which says a lot.

The house is quiet, the morning light filtering in through the front window. The front of our house gets the morning light, bathing our living room in a warm, happy greeting to the day. I love that space for that reason.

"Yes. I didn't know where you were and couldn't open your door."

"I'm sorry. I must have accidentally locked it. But I am here now. Want some breakfast?"

"I just want some milk, please."

"We can certainly make that happen," I say as I head towards the kitchen, Reeves following behind.

I open the back door as I walk into the kitchen to let Mr. Bojangles out. I leave the door open, welcoming in the fresh morning air.

"Momma. Is Grayman my dad?"

I stop in my tracks. Where is this coming from? How do I answer this? The blood flow is racing through me. I can feel the pulse thumping throughout my body. My heart is pounding out of my chest. Can I somehow avoid answering him immediately without making him feel bad for asking?

FORTY-FIVE

Grayson

6:11 am EST

"GOOD MORNING, YOU TWO."

Hollis looks like a deer in the headlights. What did I walk into?

"Good morning. Reeves and I were talking, and guess what he just asked me right before you walked in?"

"Hmmm. Let me see. He asked if he could have green eggs and ham for breakfast?"

Reeves laughs, his sweet giggle so innocent and pure. "No, silly. I asked if you are my dad."

"Oh," I respond, looking desperately at Hollis for guidance. Her eyes were already fixed on me, wide with anticipation. She tilts her head as if to say, "Answer him."

"Oh, well. Your mom and I were going to talk to you about this. I'm so glad you asked." I look over at Hollis, and she does a double nod this time. Get on with it already.

"How would you feel if I were your dad, Reeves?"

"I would like it very much. Then we can fly on your jet and go to the tall buildings and have ribbon-cutting parties."

I die at his pure, unjaded sweetness. I seriously can't take this much goodness so early in the morning. I am fighting back tears before I respond or risk embarrassing us all.

"I would like that very much, too. And guess what? You're in luck. We can do all of those things and more."

"So, you're my dad? Is he my dad, momma?"

Hollis walks over to Reeves and puts her hand on his messy, morning head of curls. "Yes, sweet love. Grayman is your dad."

"Yes!" He raises his fist as if in victory and pulls it down when he says this. He takes a big sip of milk and then stands up, pulling Hollis to me. He hugs us both, pulling the three of us together.

I wonder where this question in his mind came from. Intuition? Did he recognize the similarities? Or was it just a coincidence that I am his father? Might he have asked this of any man suddenly spending more time with him?

The good news is we don't have to fret anymore about how we will bring it up or what exactly we will say. He saved us from that. The cat is out of the bag.

I would never have thought that a woman in a terry bathrobe could be attractive, much less stunning. But once again, Hollis has proved me wrong. I would go so far as to call her a hot piece of ass, but I am trying to work on those bad words. Not to mention, I don't see her that way at all. But, damn.

"Can I call him dad?" The innocent but appropriate question breaks my train of thought. I wait for Hollis to take this one.

"You can call him whatever you like, sweetheart. Grayman, Grayson, Dad, Pop. You name it, and he will answer to it, I'm certain."

At this last part, she looks up at me and smiles. She makes it seem so easy, answering a four-year-old's deep, thought-provoking questions. I am still exhausted from the last one.

Epilogue

HOLLIS

Sunday, November 17th, 2024

Sky Zone

Kitty Hawk, NC

2:17 PM *EST*

HAPPY BIRTHDAY TO YOU. *Happy birthday to you. Happy birthday, dear Reeves. Happy birthday to you!*

Reeves is five today. We are at Sky Zone, one of those jumping places that feels like a deathtrap to me. But he begged, and Grayson can't deny him anything. He feels like he has to make up for the first four-plus years he missed.

So here we are. I am nine and a half months pregnant. Literally, I could give birth here on the trampoline or in the pool of plastic balls, and no one would probably even notice.

I was due November 11, exactly a week ago. For someone who spent so much time and effort and worry and angst over trying to get pregnant with my first husband, I sure can get pregnant faster than a bunny with Grayson.

I never went on the pill because I simply didn't even have enough time to get in to see my gynecologist before he knocked me up again. And we used a condom every time. A lot of good that did.

They say the best things come when they aren't planned. That is certainly what I am taking away from what feels like the Disney fairytale I told myself didn't exist.

I didn't have a plan for where to live when I got divorced and had to officially be out of our house in Raleigh. I met Grayson in an explosive way, and he provided me with an answer to my unplanned domicile.

Grayson didn't plan to stay at the beach house in Duck that fateful day, and things just got crazier after that. While the whole situation was a complete mess, we wouldn't have met if Claire hadn't done what she did and Grayson hadn't had a last-minute change of plans.

As a single mom, I didn't have a scheme in place for how to care for this new baby. A freak fire made that decision for me. I got to live in a resort with an entire family. They were there for me. They helped me learn how to care for this precious baby boy and filled in when I needed an extra hand.

Without even knowing it, Grayson has been picking me up when I'm down and saving me at times I didn't even know

I needed saving. He *is* my knight in shining armor.

Not long after that day in August last year, when Reeves asked if Grayson was his father, he started asking us why we weren't married. How do you explain to an almost five-year-old that even though we have known each other for at least five years, clearly, we still had so much to learn about each other?

We left that question to linger for a while, an ever-present notion because Reeves didn't let it go. On his birthday in November, a year ago today, he said his only wish is for his mom and dad to get married.

We tied the knot on the beach in front of the beach house the following month on Christmas Eve. Our families were there, including my surrogate family from The Sanderling and Sacred Grounds. It was small but filled with love, with everyone we care so much about to witness it.

Kendall and Ava were my maids of honor. Reeves was Grayson's best [little] man.

We live full-time at the beach house, but Grayson still travels often. He assures me it is far less than it used to be. But I want him with me all of the time, so it feels like a lot.

He has stepped into the role of father like he was made for it. He is patient and kind and loves playing with Reeves any chance he gets. I was always Reeves' best friend. He said so to anyone who would listen. I was demoted when Grayson came into the picture, and I am okay with that. I love watching them together.

I am still number one in Mr. Bojangles' eyes. He is an old man now at eleven. He is slower and hasn't taken down any robbers since the day Grayson and I met. He is still my protector, and I do not doubt that he would if I needed him to. He is living out his golden years lounging on the beachfront deck and taking shorter, slower walks on the beach with me.

As I sit here reflecting on the last ten years of my life, my marriage and eventual divorce, and now finding the true love of my life, I am proud of myself for surviving. I would do it all again to end up back here with my family. This is precisely where I am supposed to be. It just took some non-planned, sometimes unfortunate events to end up here.

As if out of nowhere, I feel like I wet myself. I know I didn't, but my long skirt is soaking wet. I know immediately what that means. My water has broken. Our little girl will soon arrive.

I guess I always imagined it would be less dramatic than everything that has led us to our now calm life. Children running and screaming all around me. I don't have a clue where my husband is. Will anyone even hear me if I call out?

"Grayson! She's coming!" I say, and he comes rushing toward me with Reeves.

Just like everything with us, she is coming into the world with a bang. Our baby firecracker will fit right in.

Afterword

If you liked *Billionaire Second Chance*, you will love my newest release, Pucking My Ex. Order it here.

I can't imagine anything worse than running into my hot hockey star ex in Italy.

Until a one-night-stand ups the ante with a + pregnancy test.

I expected to never see Benton Jeffries again after our messy split.

A decade passes before I lay eyes on him again at a friend's destination wedding.

He sure knows how to knock a puck in the hole.

Those piercing blue eyes and chiseled jaw should be a hooking penalty.

With all willpower officially gone, I let him in my hotel room after a day in Sorrento.

My walls come down along with my panties.

As the sun rises, reality creeps in.

I get up and book the first flight out of there.

It's a no-go with his pro hockey career in Canada, and my life in Atlanta.

But somethings gotta give when I get two little pink lines.

Did I get your attention? Read it now here.

Here is a snippet of the beginning:

Chapter One
Mary Mac

Red Line: *The red line is the horizontal line that divides the ice surface in half. It is also where the opening face occurs*

Naples, Italy

Thursday, August 10, 2023

9:12 am

I am blindly navigating the narrow cobblestone streets of the ancient Italian city. The fading sunlight casts long, narrow shadows and produces long cuts of light across the pastel-colored stucco buildings.

The air is charged with a tension I can't quite put my finger on. But my body feels it. An uncomfortable silence surrounds me. The bustling crowd I expected is nowhere to be found. I am alone in this hauntingly beautiful and eerily silent place.

The smell of freshly brewed coffee wafts through the air.

I feel the uneasiness rising up inside of me, catching at the top of my chest. I don't know why no one came to get me when they left the hotel for the wedding rehearsal.

I am irritated and panicked, worried I will be the last one walking in. When it occurred to me that I was late, I ran out of the hotel without getting directions from the hotel staff. I struggle with my Italian and didn't have time to patiently work through their broken English, panic rising.

I approach the grand cathedral. This place is exquisite. I want to pause to take it in. The soaring spires and detail work are breathtaking. Emily has always been a devout Catholic, but I could have sworn she said she wasn't getting married in a church. Everything feels off. And unsettled.

I don't have time to stop and appreciate its grandeur. I walk up the stone steps to the front doors.

As I stick my head in, the heavy, tall, arched red door creaks with an ominous groan. Am I in the right place? An extensive black and white checkerboard aisle leads the way to the front of the church.

I can hear a faint baritone voice booming from the front of the narthex, but I can't distinguish the person it's coming from. Or the language they are speaking.

I squint my eyes, straining to see as I approach the front of the empty, candlelit church. The vastness is swallowing me.

The barren aisles are adorned with dried flowers in muted colors. An unsettling stillness hangs in the air, sending a shiver through me.

My steps echo through the cavernous space as I get closer to the altar, where Emily stands in her gown, a long trail behind her. As I get closer, I realize no one else is with her. Where is everyone? Who was talking? Something isn't right, my Spidey sense tells me.

"Emily. I'm sorry I am late. Where is everyone?"

She doesn't turn around or respond as I approach her. A deep feeling of foreboding surges through me, increasing my already anxious feeling.

An unsettling quiet replaces the rushed anticipation I felt on my way here. A desire to retreat, to run away. A chill catches me as I touch her shoulder, and I shake slightly. My normally warm and affable friend doesn't turn to me. She walks away instead.

A draft, seemingly out of nowhere, extinguishes all the candles at once, plunging the cathedral into almost complete darkness. It is now illuminated only by the filtered light coming in through the gothic stained glass windows. My panic is sent into overdrive as my surroundings transform into a disorienting maze of shadows. Spots of red and yellow and blue are cast around me.

Finish reading here!

Also by Blakely Stone

Billionaire Fake Proposal

Billionaire Grumpy Daddy

Billionaire Enemy Roommate

Christmas with the Grump

Pucking My Ex

Pucking Dad's BFF

Pucking My Neighbor

Made in United States
North Haven, CT
02 July 2024

54314112R00163